She was hypnotized by Rafael's nearness

He took her chin in his hands, slowly tilting it upward. "I don't know why I worry about you, but I do," he said. Slowly he lowered his mouth, his lips pressing against Lila's with an overpowering mixture of tenderness and authority. As she felt the length of his body press against her, her breath was completely taken away. Her blood began throbbing as he tasted her lips, exciting each nerve ending. Involuntarily she twined her arms around his neck.

He pulled away then, leaving her trembling and shaken with her response to him. She averted her eyes in an attempt to mask her vulnerability. She couldn't bear for him to realize he held a special power over her....

WELCOME
TO THE WONDERFUL WORLD
OF *Harlequin Romances*

Interesting, informative and entertaining,
each Harlequin Romance portrays an appealing
and original love story. With a varied array
of settings, we may lure you on an African safari,
to a quaint Welsh village, or an exotic Riviera
location—anywhere and everywhere that adventurous
men and women fall in love.

As publishers of Harlequin Romances, we're
extremely proud of our books. Since 1949,
Harlequin Enterprises has built its publishing
reputation on the solid base of quality and
originality. Our stories are the most popular
paperback romances sold in North America; every
month, six new titles are released and sold at
nearly every book-selling store in Canada and the
United States.

A free catalog listing all Harlequin Romances
can be yours by writing to the

HARLEQUIN READER SERVICE,
(In the U.S.) 2504 West Southern Avenue, Tempe, AZ 85282
(In Canada) Stratford, Ontario, N5A 6W2

We sincerely hope you enjoy reading
this Harlequin Romance.

Yours truly,

THE PUBLISHERS
Harlequin Romances

Mayan Magic

Laura McGrath

Harlequin Books

TORONTO • NEW YORK • LONDON
AMSTERDAM • PARIS • SYDNEY • HAMBURG
STOCKHOLM • ATHENS • TOKYO • MILAN

Original hardcover edition published in 1982
by Mills & Boon Limited

ISBN 0-373-02588-2

Harlequin Romance first edition December 1983

CHAPTER ONE

LILA's grip on the arms of her seat tightened as the descending plane suddenly dropped into an air pocket. In her twenty years she hadn't flown enough to be able to take occasional turbulence in her stride. Hoping the airport was by now in sight, she turned to look out of the small window to her left. She was disappointed to find that the clouds still obscured the ground, as they had for the past hour of the flight. In her mind, she pictured the Yucatan Peninsula as a broad, unbroken jungle. Soon, she hoped, she would be able to see how closely it matched her expectations.

She glanced inconspicuously at the man who had taken the empty seat beside her about an hour before. Steve Taylor was not the sort of man she found appealing, although no doubt many women would think he was quite handsome. Lila found his finely shaped features and wavy golden hair a bit too perfect. Still, he was friendly and full of boyish charm. As it turned out, their fathers had both gone to the same medical school. It felt strange to be so far away from home and meet someone even remotely connected to her.

Beneath the last translucent cloud layer, she made out the long grey runway at Merida Airport.

It was surrounded on all sides by what appeared to be dense jungle, broken by an occasional stone structure or thatched hut. A momentary feeling of panic stabbed upward from the pit of her stomach. Her last-minute decision to come here to paint the ruins had left her little time to worry, and she had seen the trip as an exciting adventure as well as a favour to a friend. Now that she could see for herself how primitive this land was, she had second thoughts about the wisdom of coming here on her own.

When Jonathan had begged her to serve as a replacement for a painter who had suffered a heart attack, he had been desperate. He had planned a department store display with paintings of the ruins as the central theme, and it would fall through if Lila refused to help him. Always dramatic, Jonathan had insisted that she held his career in her hands. So Lila, against the advice of her friends, had goodnaturedly agreed to make the trip. Certainly it was exciting to break away from familiar surroundings, but maybe this time she had carried her natural helpfulness too far.

Quelling her nervousness, she turned back from the window, to find Steve writing his name and telephone number on the back of a business card.

'You look a little scared about this trip, if you ask me. Here, take this card, and give me a call if you decide to take me up on my offer of a guided tour.'

Lila turned over the card and found 'Mayan

Holiday Tours: Uxmal, Chichen Itza, Tikal' engraved on the front.

'I'm headed to Chichen first, but then I'll be in Uxmal. Where will you be staying? Or is that a secret?' He grinned engagingly.

Lila blushed slightly. 'No, it's not a secret at all. But the truth is, I'm not certain. I have the name of a hotel in Uxmal, but I'm not sure I'll be staying there. So I guess I'll have to be the one to call you.'

Steve gave a resigned shrug; and Lila could read the disappointment in his face.

'You won't find a better guide for the ruins, I can promise you. I had to take a six-week course before leading my first tour, and this is my second season at it.'

Lila found it hard to overcome a feeling of re-assuring an eager puppy. 'I believe you. I'll be sure to call if I want a tour.' Privately, she was relieved that she hadn't been able to give him a telephone number or address. Something in Steve's manner made her aware that there was more than ordinary friendliness behind his offer.

She had lots of work ahead of her and couldn't really afford to be distracted. Still, if she had known where she was staying she would have felt obliged to tell him. Lila had little experience in avoiding unwanted male attentions and had never learned how to do this gracefully.

The stewardess announced the beginning of their final descent into Merida, and passengers began buckling their seat-belts in preparation for landing. Lila searched in her leather shoulder bag for her cosmetics to take advantage of the few minutes remaining.

Gazing absently into her small mirror, she combed her heavy, honey-blonde hair until it rested smoothly on her shoulders. Her turquoise-blue eyes stared back at her from the mirror, somewhat clouded by worry. She noted the frown that had appeared on her forehead and made an effort to relax as she freshened her pale bronze lipstick.

Holding the mirror farther away from her face, she tried to imagine how she would look to the people of Uxmal. At home, people often said she had a face like a pixie. Lila would have preferred something more grand and mature, but she knew her small frame and pointed chin gave an impression of someone childlike and cute, even though her figure was decidedly womanly.

The bump of the plane's wheels on the runway announced their arrival in Merida. Lila was a bit surprised that the plane had landed so quickly and she hurried to replace her mirror in her bag. The level of conversation among the passengers stepped up noticeably as people began unbuckling their seat-belts and gathering up their belongings in preparation for disembarking.

Steve stepped into the aisle, leaving a place for Lila in front of him. With a smile of thanks, she moved into the line of passengers and hurried eagerly down the stairs into the bright, hot afternoon. In spite of the partial cloud cover, the sun was blazing overhead and the heat momentarily took her breath away.

By the time she had made her way to the baggage area, the carousel was beginning its mechanical limp along the circular track. As Lila was reaching for her one pale blue leather suitcase, she glanced up just in time to observe her aqua and white checked canvas bag come toppling over the ridge, noisily spilling its contents on to the metal ring. She flushed a deep pink as everyone turned to watch the skittering paints, brushes, and canvas boards begin their slow, separate journeys around the circle. Lila stood paralysed for a moment, reluctant to identify herself as the owner of the bag by stepping forward to claim its contents.

By the time her scattered possessions began a second trip around the carousel, most of the bystanders had lost interest in the incident and had returned to gathering up their own belongings. Lila had regained some of her composure and began the task of hurriedly stuffing her supplies back into the bag. By filling both hands, she managed to capture the canvas boards and most of the small tubes of paint before they moved out of reach. She decided to wait for the next round to retrieve the brushes, so that she wouldn't be in the ridiculous position of running alongside the carousel picking off the few remaining items.

'I think these are yours, aren't they?' a feminine voice enquired, and Lila looked up to see a magnificently groomed woman, perhaps in her early forties, smiling and holding out her paintbrushes. Her artist's eye automatically noted the woman's hands—long tapering fingers, nails beautifully manicured and polished, and on the third finger a large ring with an opal surrounded by the glitter of diamonds. The exotic-looking woman had shining black hair, high cheekbones, and large eyes, emphasised by skilful use of cosmetics.

'Is painting your hobby?' the woman asked in a throaty tone.

'It's my full-time profession,' Lila answered, raising her chin proudly.

'Indeed, *chérie*, and what brings you to the Yucatan?'

Lila thought she detected a slight accent in the woman's speech, but she couldn't put her finger on what it might be. Her features were more European than American, she thought. But perhaps she was just expecting her to be foreign because of her sophisticated appearance.

'I've come down to do some paintings of the Mayan ruins at Uxmal,' she answered, somewhat flustered at discussing her plans with such an obviously cosmopolitan woman.

'That's wonderful, my dear! I live just outside Uxmal myself. Will you be staying with friends?'

'Well, I was going to try the Hacienda Hermosa . . .'

A husky laugh interrupted her. 'My dear, I'm sorry, but you must have got that name out of an old guidebook. The Hacienda Hermosa used to be quite charming, if a little primitive. But it's been going downhill lately and it's no place for an attractive young woman to stay alone. In any case, I doubt you could get a room there. Some house guests of mine enquired at all the local places a few days ago, and there wasn't a thing available.'

Lila's heart sank. From the sound of things, she wouldn't be able to stay in Uxmal at all.

'Have you done much travelling alone?' the woman asked with a slight frown.

Lila was tempted for a moment to exaggerate her experience. She hated to appear naïve to her new acquaintance, but perhaps this was an opportunity to receive some helpful advice. 'This is the first time I've been away from home by myself,' she confessed with an embarrassed smile.

'I see,' the woman said slowly, seeming to consider a moment. 'Why don't you stay at my house for a while? I've just said goodbye to my house guests, and I would appreciate the company.'

Lila could hardly believe her ears. Surely her acquaintance wasn't serious? She summoned her manners and smiled at the woman. 'Thank you, it's very kind of you. But I couldn't impose on you like that.'

'Of course you will stay with me! You are alone, and I too am alone. You'll need someone to show you around. I own an art gallery here, and I always have a spare bedroom ready to offer young artists who need a place to stay. And frankly, I would never forgive myself for letting you wander off alone without promise of a hotel room.'

The woman's insistence dissolved Lila's fears of intruding and she found herself agreeing to the plan. This woman really seemed to want her company, and it was pleasant to feel that she wasn't totally on her own.

'I'll fetch my car while you go through Customs,' the woman announced, searching in her pale snakeskin purse for her keys. 'We can meet outside. I'll be driving a red Peugeot.'

Lila nodded and then moved to take her place in a line to go through Customs. Suddenly a stunning brunette in a cerise silk dress pushed to the front of the next line, seemingly oblivious to the outraged looks and mutterings of those she had displaced. Lila could not help admiring the woman's perfect model's figure, accented by her closely fitting dress. It was a pity her physical beauty was not matched by her courtesy, Lila thought as the brunette hissed impatiently at a porter who had placed her luggage at the end of the line.

The woman continued her tirade as her bags were placed before the Customs officer, Lila noted. She refused to open her suitcases, forcing the official to open them for her. His cursory inspection of her belongings was accompanied by a shrill protest. 'I don't have time for this nonsense!

I'm well known here. Besides, I'm in a hurry—someone is meeting me outside.' The brunette finally regained her luggage and left with a porter, remarking loudly, 'My friend is a very important man in this area. If he knew I was being pestered by petty bureaucrats, he'd see that something was done about it, I assure you!'

Lila breathed a sigh of relief at the woman's departure, and quietly completed her own Customs procedures. She collected her bags and walked out beyond the overhanging roof to the kerb. Once outside the air-conditioned airport, she was amazed at the intensity of the heat. It was a good thing she had brought her most summery outfits. Already the sun was burning through the eyelet pattern in her white cotton blouse. The palm trees and oleanders which surrounded the airport combined with the heat to make her realise that she had actually arrived in the tropics.

As Lila watched for her new friend, she caught sight of a darkly handsome man pulling up to the kerb in a white Mercedes. The brunette she had seen in Customs rushed to the car, gesturing gracefully to the porter to bring her bags. The driver of the car loaded her luggage in the trunk and, as he opened the door for her, he glanced in Lila's direction. For a brief moment their eyes met, then he closed the door and turned away. Lila was somehow disappointed that such a handsome man should be meeting such an unpleasant woman.

She had been waiting at the kerb for several minutes when a shining scarlet Peugeot pulled up alongside her. While the engine continued to purr, her hostess slid gracefully out of the driver's seat and opened the spacious trunk. A nearby porter hurried over to place Lila's bags inside and collect his tip. As the car drew smoothly away from the airport, the woman gave Lila a quick smile, saying, 'Forgive me, I should have introduced myself much sooner. After all, here you are in a strange place being whisked off by someone you don't even know. I'm Françoise Miguel. Call me Françoise, of course. And you?'

'Lila Fleming,' she answered, a little surprised at the relief she felt finally to know her hostess's name. So her guess about the woman being European was apparently correct, she mused, basking in the air-conditioned luxury of the car. She was probably from Paris, judging from her sophisticated dress. As she seemed to concentrate on her driving, which was skilful if a bit too fast, Lila gazed entranced out the window. She wanted to absorb as much of this new land as she could during the drive to Françoise's house. Still in town, they drove on a broad, four-lane road parted down the centre by a row of miniature palms. Along the side of the road, discreetly modern one-storey buildings occasionally appeared amid the dense greenery. Every few miles Françoise would give wide berth to a moped carrying a young man with a load of food or other cargo tied to the seat behind him.

Once past the city limits, the verdant covering of sisal—the major cash crop of the Yucatan—became unceasing. It was interrupted only occasionally by a giant windmill whirling against the pastel sky, or by a peasant's home, made from limestone or palm leaves. In the distance, the broad flat terrain was flanked on both sides by smooth, low-lying mountains, which were also a bright chartreuse. Their rounded shapes and even covering of grasses made them look like soft green pillows.

Françoise relaxed back into the soft leather seat and turned to Lila.

'Tell me, what made you choose Uxmal to paint?'

'A friend of mine is putting together a promotion on ancient cultures for a local department store. It's to go along with a new line of fashions. The painter whose work he was going to use couldn't come, and he asked me to fill in by doing several paintings for the show. So here I am.'

'That's quite a compliment. Your parents must be very proud of you, no?'

'Er—I guess so,' Lila responded lamely. She felt a moment's temptation to tell Françoise that her mother had died two years ago, and that her father, being a highly successful surgeon, was kept quite busy between his work and the local widows. But she stopped herself. Even though Françoise seemed warm and friendly, she was probably not interested in the details of Lila's family.

Actually, Lila thought, she wished she could believe her father was proud of her. He seemed to be preoccupied most of the time, but he had made his disapproval of her chosen career apparent. He would rather she had selected something much more practical than art. He said artists were dreamers, always living on the fringes of society.

Lila's forehead wrinkled as she stared down at the sterling silver bracelet her father and mother had given her on her eighteenth birthday. Her mother might have been proud of her if she were still alive. But she probably would have thought Lila foolish to make this trip. And deep inside, Lila knew she was taking a chance. Jonathan was forever involved in schemes which fell through more often than not. Lila sighed. Still, if Françoise really owned a gallery, she might not have to rely solely on Jonathan's plan to show her work. She could hardly believe her good fortune. Here she was on her way to Uxmal, with a place to stay in the home of the sophisticated owner of an art gallery. A feeling of excitement rose in her as she began to realise all the new experiences she would be having.

The next several miles were driven in silence, until they approached what appeared to be an English country estate set on a grassy knoll. Lila's eyes widened in shock at the incongruity of seeing this mansion in a place where she had come to expect thatched huts and small stucco structures.

Could this be Françoise's house?

'Who lives there, Françoise?' she asked, as the car passed the drive without slowing.

'Quite a place, eh? It belongs to Rafael Cornejo Blake. It's Palmera House, the old family estate. His grandfather came here from England in the early part of the century and he had it built for his Spanish bride. The estate is maintained by the staff. One never knows what part of the world Rafael is in, but I guess he always returns to Uxmal for part of the year. They say it's his favourite place.'

'You don't know him, then?'

'No. He's not an easy man to get to know. I live not more than a mile from him, but I've seen him only a few times, and then quite by accident. We don't travel in the same circles, and people say he leads a very private life.'

The Peugeot turned sharply to the left and on to a dirt path with overhanging laurel trees. The path continued for perhaps half a mile before reaching a large two-storey house made of hand-cut stone and wide expanses of glass. The windows shimmered like mirrors in the bright sun.

Françoise plunked down Lila's bags on the marble floors of the entryway. 'I'll ring for Rosa to take your cases to the guestroom, *chérie*, so that you can take a little siesta. Later this afternoon there's to be the party of the season. I'd like to show you off if you're not too tired from your trip. New faces are uncommon here in our little community—especially pretty ones.'

A stout, dark-skinned woman with prominent cheekbones and large almond-shaped eyes appeared silently in the hall. She curtsied slightly as Françoise introduced her to Lila, then startled Lila with a broad maternal smile. 'I see we must feed you well here. You are just a little thin.' Rosa held up her thumb and forefinger to demonstrate and looked to Françoise for confirmation.

Françoise laughed gaily. 'It's true, Lila, that the local standards favour plumpness. But I think you'll pass inspection.'

Tiptoeing slightly ahead, Rosa ushered her into the room at the far end of the winding upstairs hall. Not having seen the rest of the house, Lila was completely unprepared for the elegance that greeted her. Although she had pictured it in her daydreams, in real life she had never seen a bed like the one before her. Delicately gathered on the brass frame surrounding the queen-sized bed was a diaphanous organdie curtain. The bed-covers were all white, save the hand-embroidered roses on the linen pillowcases.

Next to the bed was a round glass-topped table with two overlapping skirts—the top and shorter one of Irish linen, the underneath, a floor-length skirt of delicately patterned chintz. Lila recognised the vase full of roses on the tabletop as the source of the rich perfume that wafted through the air. A kidney-shaped dressing-table with matching skirt was on her left between two glass doors which opened on to a narrow veranda. And on her right was a carved walnut dresser with a triptych mirror in the style of Louis XV.

Lila gulped in silent amazement, and Rosa smiled proudly. 'This is my favourite room in the house. I hope you will be comfortable in it.' Rosa set her bags down in front of the dresser, and slipped out, closing the door softly behind her.

Lila quickly stripped off her travelling clothes and drew a bath in the elegant pink-tiled bathroom that adjoined the room. Noticing a collection of foaming bath oils and scented soaps on a wicker shelf, she added a few drops of jasmine oil to the bath before she stepped in. She leaned back in the warm, lightly perfumed water, letting it lap softly over her skin. As she inhaled the fragrance of the bath oil, the morning's events swirled in her head.

She couldn't believe her good fortune in meeting Françoise. And imagine having such an elegant place to stay! She had to admit she was less than enthusiastic about going to the party this afternoon. Françoise had said it was the social event of the year, which made all sorts of questions pop into her head. What was the occasion? Who would be there? She had a sudden, disquieting memory of the handsome man who had met the brunette at the airport, then her thoughts turned back to the party. What should she wear? Her stomach was starting to flutter at the thought of meeting a group of distinguished, wealthy strangers.

She was often a little shy at social gatherings, even when she knew everyone. Here she wouldn't know a soul, except Françoise. But, she thought drowsily, it seemed that Françoise wanted her to go, and that was the least she could do in recognition of her hospitality.

She slowly patted herself dry with a huge fluffy pink and white towel, even while enjoying the cool sensation of the air against her moist naked skin. Then, putting on a light cotton wrap, she sank drowsily on to the bed. She was awakened from her nap by a soft knock at the door and the clink of a glass of iced tea being placed on the nightstand.

'Señora said she would like to see you before it's time to get ready for the party. She's on the veranda having her tea.'

'What time does the party start?'

'Not until three-thirty, I think. You still have a couple of hours,' Rosa added as she left the room.

Lila slipped into a pair of comfortable white cotton slacks and a short-sleeved chartreuse tee-shirt, stepped into her low-heeled sandals, and went downstairs to find her hostess.

From the entry hall, she spotted Françoise on the veranda. She crossed through a lavishly appointed dining room, pausing to admire the Mexican primitive paintings hung on the walls. Françoise caught sight of her and gestured an invitation, smiling broadly.

'Hello, my dear. I was beginning to think I would be going to the party without you,' she teased.

Now that the party was only a couple of hours away, Lila was anxious to know more about it. As airily as possible, she asked, 'What do you think the party will be like?'

Sensing her uneasiness, Françoise was eager to reassure her. 'Of course, you must be curious about the party. It's to celebrate the opening of a new free medical clinic in Uxmal. Everyone involved in the development of the clinic will be there this afternoon. Come to think of it, I guess that takes in all the socially prominent families in and around Uxmal. Most of the money for the clinic came from an anonymous donor, but almost everyone had some part to play. I myself arranged for the decoration of the lobby and the children's examining rooms. Of course Rafael, my mysterious neighbour, remained aloof as usual. Still, I hear he has agreed to attend the party. I think this will be the first time we attend the same event.'

Lila had to think for a moment before she remembered who Françoise was referring to. Then she recalled that Rafael was the man who lived in that grand English mansion they had passed on the way from the airport. She pictured a well-dressed, distinguished-looking man with silver hair, and felt a churn of anxiety in her stomach.

It was frightful enough to be brought into a group of strangers, much less into such a seemingly aristocratic circle. Even though her parents had had a busy social life which included many formal gatherings, Lila herself had never really taken part in them. Brushing her hair back nervously, she looked down at her simple cotton slacks and sandals.

'What clothes did you bring, my dear?' Françoise had apparently been reading her last thought.

'Er—well,' Lila stammered.

'Some of the women will be overdressed, of course. The same ones will use every opportunity to show off their new gowns. Like Mrs Reynaldo . . . Well, no matter. Most of the women will wear tasteful cotton dresses and sandals, and there will probably be one or two in lightweight slacks.'

Lila breathed a sigh of relief at hearing that the party would not be formal.

'You probably have at least one dress in your suitcase, *n'est-ce pas?*' Françoise's eyes twinkled as she cocked her head to one side.

'I wasn't sure I would have any occasion to wear them, but I did bring two dresses.'

'Good. Rosa can press them for you if they need it. But no need to worry. You will look like an angel no matter what you are wearing.'

Lila lowered her lashes. She had never thought of herself as being particularly attractive. Somehow she had always felt overshadowed by her mother's radiant beauty. As a child she had often been told by adults that she would be lucky to grow up to be as lovely as her mother. But she didn't look very much like her, so compliments like the one she had just received always took her by surprise.

Lila and Françoise chatted idly until it was time to get ready for the party. Lila removed both her dresses from her suitcase. Which would be best? she wondered. The white square-necked dress was certainly becoming, and it should set off her tan. But, she thought, it would look a little young in a gathering of older people. The yellow was more sophisticated and would make it a little easier to blend into the crowd.

Lila remembered the only time she had put it on. It was outrageously expensive and she had had to save for a long time to buy it. She had planned to wear it to a small dinner party to celebrate a successful showing of a friend's sculptures. But her father, who happened to come home early that evening, had considered the dress too revealing and had coldly suggested that she wear something else. And as usual, Lila thought ruefully, she had given in to him immediately, hoping for his approval. It was a relief to be on her own here, able to make her own decisions without trying to please her father. Nevertheless, she did feel a little like a rudderless ship.

She slipped on the lemon yellow dress. Its cotton jersey fabric softly hugged the curves of her slender figure and the colour contrasted appealingly with her tanned skin. She took out the topaz pendant that had been her mother's favourite and fastened it around her neck. Casting a critical eye at the neckline of her dress, which revealed the gentle upper curves of her breasts, she lifted her chin with a hint of defiance.

Before joining her hostess, she gave herself one last inspection in the mirror. Her hair was responding to the humidity, and her elfin features were framed by small ringlets of new hair. She had selected a brown eyeshadow, but now that she saw how it enlarged her eyes, she wondered briefly if perhaps she should have chosen a lighter shade, more along the lines of her pale, toffee-coloured lipstick. Her gaze passed approvingly over the dress and down to her delicate high-heeled sandals. Then the sound of Françoise's high heels clicking on the tiles of the entryway suggested it was time to make her appearance downstairs. Taking a deep breath, she collected her small clutch purse from the chair and went down to meet her hostess.

Françoise exclaimed with delight as she turned to see Lila coming towards her. 'My dear, you look absolutely stunning! No doubt you'll have all the men eager to make your acquaintance. I used to wear Jean Chac dresses myself when I was your age.' She looked down and gave a cursory pat to her hips. 'But I must say, I never looked like you do in them. The dress looks as though it were made for you. With your complexion, you don't even need make-up,' Françoise remarked admiringly, putting her silver cigarette case and lighter in a small beaded bag. Lila put her hands to her cheeks, which were flushed and warm from nervous anticipation.

Françoise gave her a sympathetic look. 'Don't worry, I'll be sure to introduce you to everyone, and you'll find the people very friendly.'

Climbing into the red Peugeot, Lila vowed to try to relax and enjoy herself at the party. Even if she did turn out to be the only young person there, as she feared, there was no real reason to feel awkward or selfconscious. Despite the fact that she was in a strange country where she knew almost no one, there was no reason to expect this party to be different from any other.

CHAPTER TWO

AFTER a ten-minute drive on the main road, Françoise made a sharp turn on to a gravelled, winding track. As Lila heard the faint sound of mariachi music, pangs of nervousness assailed her and she gripped her purse a little more firmly. The Peugeot came to rest at the end of the driveway, where a group of European cars were haphazardly arranged. On the wide, immaculately kept front lawn, a few men and women were engaged in a game of croquet. Françoise gestured greetings to several of her friends as she and Lila made their way to the front entrance.

Some of her tension dissolved when she saw that, at least as far as her dress was concerned, she had nothing to worry about. Françoise had been right, she thought, and breathed a small sigh of relief.

Françoise appeared to know almost everyone at the party, and Lila followed her from one small knot of people to another. Surprised at how welcoming and friendly everyone was to her, she felt herself begin to relax and have fun. She was glad Françoise had wanted to bring her; she never would have had the opportunity to meet such interesting people if she had been staying in a hotel.

She was talking with a nurse who would be working in the new clinic when she noticed a sudden crescendo in the surrounding conversation, and glancing towards the entryway, she saw the same darkly handsome man escorting the beautiful brunette he had met at the airport. Now Lila saw that the man was over six feet tall, with broad shoulders and jet black hair. The woman clung possessively to his arm. Her long slender legs and tanned skin provided a perfect showcase for the offwhite jumpsuit that daringly hugged her willowy frame. A red cloisonné comb held her thick dark hair just behind one ear.

As the man introduced the brunette to those nearby, the conversations began to resume their former pitch. Lila couldn't help wondering about the identity of the couple, whom she had seen twice in the few hours since she had arrived. Glancing at them a few minutes later, her eyes again met the man's direct look and she sensed that he had been observing her. Unaccountably embarrassed, she turned her attention quickly to the woman at her side. Mrs Bennett was in the midst of telling several people about last year's fiesta, when the grand prize turned out to be a live goat.

'And you should have seen Mr Blake's expression when he was presented with the prize!' She gestured dramatically and her hand bumped into Lila's glass of punch, spilling most of it down the front of her yellow dress.

'Oh, I'm terribly sorry. It was so clumsy of me.'

'It's all right,' Lila replied graciously. 'I'm sure it will come out.' She found her way to the kitchen and began busily scrubbing the front of her dress with cold water, trying not to get in the way of several bustling servants.

'It would be a shame to ruin such a beautiful dress,' a male voice observed in a slightly mocking tone.

'Oh!' Lila flushed a deep pink as she turned to find the man she had seen at the entrance standing two feet away and regarding her with amused dark eyes. He wore hand-tailored beige linen slacks, and a blue shirt open at the neck. A lock of his dark hair had strayed into the middle of his broad forehead.

'I don't believe we've met. I'm Rafael Blake. And you?'

Scarlet rose higher in her cheeks as she recognised the name. From what she had heard about Rafael Blake, she would never have considered the possibility that he was the man she had seen at the airport. She had somehow expected Rafael Blake to be a much older man. But from all appearances, he couldn't be much over thirty. And far from being a dignified elderly gentleman, he seemed to radiate masculine vitality and strength. Lila wished she could for once be more cool and poised. It was typical of her, she thought, to be meeting an attractive man in such unflattering circumstances.

'I'm Lila Fleming,' she told him, trying her best to avoid a stammer that would give away her embarrassment. 'Mrs Bennett accidentally spilled punch on my dress . . . I was just trying to wash it out.' She bit her lip, realising that she had just stated the obvious.

'Yes, I can see that.' His firm mouth curled into a sort of crooked grin. He was clearly amused by her embarrassment. 'I'm afraid that happens now and then—someone or other is bound to have a little too much to drink. But I'm surprised that it's happening at this early hour.'

'Oh no, it wasn't like that at all,' she said, feeling she had thoughtlessly damaged Mrs Bennett's reputation. 'It was just that she was telling a story and gesturing with her hands. In fact, the story was about you, when you won a live goat at the fiesta.'

He threw his head back in hearty laughter, and Lila felt herself grinning in response. 'Oh, that. Yes, I was taken completely by surprise. If I had known what the prize was going to be, I would never have entered the contest.' The twinkle left his eyes as the scene gradually faded from his mind, and he regarded Lila squarely. She tensed, feeling as if he were about to test her. 'But it sounds as if you've heard enough about me. What brings you to this local celebration? I would guess that you're someone's niece or granddaughter from more civilised surroundings.' His eyes slowly travelled the length of her slender figure, openly savouring the journey.

Lila could feel the heat rising in her cheeks again. This man's confidence and easy flirtation robbed her of whatever self-assurance she had and made her feel like an awkward schoolgirl. She noticed the appreciation in his gaze, but at the same time she felt he was laughing at her. He leaned a little closer to her, awaiting her reply, and Lila was startled to feel her heart begin to pound.

'No. I'm staying with Françoise Miguel. You probably know her . . . at least, she knows who you are.'

The warmth drained from his dark eyes, and his jaws clenched tightly. Lila felt as though an arctic wind had found its way into her idyllic jungle.

'I see,' he replied curtly. With eyes slightly narrowed, he asked slowly, 'How well do you know Señora Miguel?'

Lila was at a loss to understand this sudden coldness and, not knowing how to respond, decided to ignore it. 'Not very well at all. As a matter of fact, I just met her at the airport this afternoon, and she kindly offered to have me stay a few days with her.'

The thundercloud in Rafael's eyes became even more menacing. 'Do you make a habit of moving in with people you know nothing about? Or did you just recognise that you were birds of a feather?' His tone was full of derision.

'Just what do you mean by that?' Lila shot back, her eyes flashing with anger. 'And what right do you have to grill me like this? I can stay where I like.' She was dimly aware that her angry reaction was due as much to her own apprehension about staying with a complete stranger as it was to Rafael's arrogance.

'I mean by that, Miss Fleming, that in associating with someone of dubious reputation, you are likely to acquire that reputation for your own—unless perhaps you have earned it independently.'

Lila pressed her lips together in anger. In one sweep he had managed to insult both her and Françoise, and she didn't know which angered her more. 'You know absolutely nothing about me,' she sputtered, 'and as for Françoise . . .'

'Am I interrupting something?' The cool feminine voice belonged to the woman who had come with Rafael. She was standing at the kitchen door. And, although her remarks were addressed to Rafael, she was regarding Lila with an unfriendly glare.

He swung around to face her. 'Stephanie! No, you're not interrupting anything. This is Lila Fleming. Lila, Stephanie Marshall.'

'H-How do you do,' said Lila, her voice still shaking with emotion. Stephanie acknowledged her with a slight nod, and turned swiftly to Rafael.

'I'm ready to leave, Rafael. Can't we go now?' she said, smiling sweetly.

'Yes, we can. I think Miss Fleming was just wishing she could get rid of me, but was too polite to say so.' A sardonic grin crossed his face. Stephanie slipped her slender fingers under his arm as they went in search of the hostess to say their goodbyes.

Lila was still stinging over Rafael Blake's insults. But there was more to her reaction than anger. The encounter had been strangely disturbing. She felt as if she had been looked over and found wanting. Clearly a man with a girl-friend as beautiful as Stephanie Marshall wouldn't be interested in talking to someone like Lila.

A frown angled her brows as she thought over the conversation. What did Rafael Blake mean when he referred to Françoise as having—what was it?—a dubious reputation. She thought over all she knew about Françoise. It wasn't a great deal, she had to admit. Françoise had said she had married a much older man. He had been ill for several years before leaving her a wealthy widow. Now she wanted to have a good time, enjoying herself without being tied down by responsibilities. A little frivolous, perhaps. But Rafael's comment implied something more serious. Well, she wasn't going to spend her time trying to decipher his insults.

Lila looked down at her dress and saw that although it had dried completely, she could still make out a faint dark circle. Maybe it would come out with a proper washing. She left the kitchen, found Françoise, and accompanied her on a few more rounds of animated conversation before the crowd began to thin noticeably. Since her talk with Rafael Blake, Lila had been unable to concentrate on other conversations, and she was relieved when Françoise finally announced that she was ready to leave.

'Well, how did you find the party, my dear?' Françoise enquired as they made the turn on to the paved road. Without waiting for a reply, she went on, 'I was right, you know. Everyone was coming up to me and telling me what a lovely young woman you are. I almost became the centre of attention—by association, of course,' she laughed.

'I'm glad to hear that, Françoise, and it's nice of you to tell me.' Lila paused. 'But apparently the high opinion of me wasn't unanimous.'

Françoise looked over with questioning eyes. 'What do you mean?'

'Rafael Blake, for instance.' Lila struggled to sound casual.

'Oh,' Françoise replied, her voice rising and falling in a sing-song, 'so you met Mr Blake. Well, if he has a low opinion of you, you're not alone. I've heard rumours that he disapproves of me too. He thinks I'm a bit too free with my favours, apparently.' She gave Lila a conspiratorial smile.

So that was his objection to Françoise, Lila

thought. Although Françoise seemed amused by
his disapproval, Lila felt a little embarrassed that
the other woman seemed to find no reason to
quarrel with Rafael Blake's assessment of her. To
change the subject, she said, 'I also met Stephanie
Marshall, the women who came to the party with
him. She wasn't very friendly to me, but she
seemed quite attached to Rafael Blake.'

'I don't know who she is. But I wouldn't be
surprised if she were after him. He is considered
the most eligible bachelor within several hundred
miles. I would be interested myself if I were once
more young and looking for money. He has a certain appeal, but he's too serious for my tastes. And
in any case, I think we have different outlooks on
life. But you . . .' her eyes twinkled at Lila, 'you
are young and innocent—just what he wants. He's
a strange one but undoubtedly a good catch, if
you know what I mean.'

Lila shrank at the suggestion that she pursue
this Rafael Blake. For one thing, she could never
be that aggressive or calculating. And certainly
she could never marry for money, as Françoise
seemed to be suggesting. If she were to marry,
she would have to love someone—really love him;
and so far, she had never met anyone she felt that
way about. Besides, Rafael Blake was obviously
opinionated and arrogant. And the sooner he was
out of her mind, the better. 'I'm really not interested in Rafael Blake,' she replied evenly.

Françoise manoeuvred the Peugeot into her

circular drive. Rosa had left the front light on for
them and Lila noticed Françoise's Himalayan cat
wandering sleepily out from under a hibiscus bush
to greet his mistress.

'Would you like a little sherry before retiring,
my dear? I think I'm going to have a glass while I
put my feet up for a few minutes.'

'No, thanks, Françoise. I'm pretty tired. I think
I'll go straight up to bed. Goodnight.'

Lila quietly hung her clothes in the bedroom
closet as she thought over the day's events. In the
last few hours she had met the most handsome
man she had ever seen. She could see how a
beautiful woman like Stephanie Marshall would
be attracted to him. After all, if Françoise was
right about his being the most eligible bachelor
around, he must have a flock of beautiful women
at his beck and call. In fact, maybe it was having
a flock of women after him that made him so
arrogant. She was suddenly aware that she was
still feeling angry over his gratuitous insults. She
should be concentrating on the paintings Jonathan
needed, she realised irritably, but her mind kept
straying to her meeting with Rafael Blake.

Rosa had thoughtfully laid out her nightgown
and turned down her bed. Lila crawled in, nuzzl-
ing her cheek against the cool pillowcase, and
went to sleep immediately.

CHAPTER THREE

THE next morning, Lila awoke early. It looked as if it was going to be a gorgeous sunny day, and she was eager to get started with her work. Downstairs she found Rosa busy in the large kitchen, which had a lovely view of the garden and pool. The room was filled with the aroma of fresh coffee.

Rosa looked surprised to see her. 'You're up early this morning, *señorita*. I'll set a place for you in the dining room. The coffee is just ready.'

'Can't I just eat here at the kitchen table?' Lila asked. 'I'd hate to eat all by myself in the big dining room.'

With a nod, Rosa set a hand-painted mug of steaming coffee on the table in front of Lila.

'Is Françoise up yet?' Lila asked.

'Oh no. Señora is usually a late sleeper. You'll be alone in the mornings, I guess.'

'Oh, that's fine,' Lila reassured her, as she took a sip of the strong coffee. 'I have lots of work to do, and I'd like to get started.'

Rosa moved about the kitchen deftly managing the eggs and bacon while she prepared a plate of fresh mango and papaya.

'I wouldn't go to the ruins today if I were you,

señorita. On Saturday and Sunday they're usually overrun by busloads of tourists. I'd wait until a weekday when it's less crowded.'

'Oh, I'd completely forgotten that this is the weekend.' She puzzled a moment, then decided it was probably a good idea not to start out on the ruins anyway. She could profit by spending some time absorbing the atmosphere of the Yucatan before she tried to capture the spirit of the ruins.

'Is there some place around here I might set up my easel and do some painting of the country-side?'

'Let's see . . .' Rosa slid the eggs on to Lila's plate and set the strips of bacon alongside. 'As a matter of fact, I think there is something you might like to paint, and it's not more than a mile from here. It's called a *cenote*; the ancients used them as reservoirs, and it's a lovely setting.' Rosa took a napkin and sketched the simple directions. Eager to get to work, Lila didn't linger over her breakfast. She packed her bag with a selection of paints and charcoals and set off.

The first part of the walk was on the two-lane paved road that led into Uxmal proper. It was straight and level, with low, thick woods on both sides. After a few minutes she came upon an old Indian man seated on a woven stool with pieces of handmade pottery spread out before him. He was vigorously bargaining with a tourist half in English and half in Spanish, but looked up to give Lila a friendly, toothless grin as she passed.

The road she turned off on was unmarked by any signs, and was hardly more than a bridle path. No wonder Rosa said there wouldn't be any tourists up here! she thought. The path was heavily shaded and offered welcome relief from the rays of the sun, already strong although midday was still hours away. Stone steps had been placed into the last several feet of the path as it steepened its angle to a ridge above, and Lila's breathing quickened as she climbed the last few feet. She wasn't used to vigorous exertion in such heat and humidity.

As she stepped on to the ridge, a flock of toucans with huge pink bills and bright yellow chests flew through the tops of the trees, their frog-like croaks piercing the silence. Surveying the setting, Lila understood immediately why Rosa had directed her here. She looked down into a deep natural basin filled with water. Vines and ferns embraced the steep terraced walls which rose above the water. A light cloud of dust on the water was made visible by the rays of the sun, but underneath the fluid was crystal, and she could see all the way to the bottom.

Lila was delighted by the serene beauty of the scene and after resting a few moments began walking along the ridge looking for a good spot to set up her easel. She had gone no more than fifty feet when she thought she heard a voice. She couldn't be sure; the sound was very soft. As she stopped and listened more intently, she recognised the sound as the humming of a child. She followed the tuneless sound to a young boy of seven or eight. He was seated against a large boulder, and was sketching something on to a notepad on his lap. The boy had dark hair and fine, aristocratic features, an unusually attractive child. Neither his face nor his dusty play clothes gave a clue to his nationality, so she wasn't sure how to greet him.

'Hello,' she said a little tentatively as she approached.

'*Ay carumba!* Now it's gone,' he exclaimed angrily.

'What's gone?'

'The iguana I was sketching.' His bottom lip protruded slightly. 'I think you scared him. They scare pretty easy, you know.'

'I'm sorry. Maybe another one will come along. May I see what you've done so far?'

He handed her the drawing, and Lila drew in a sharp breath. She was astonished at its quality, considering the youth of the artist. All in pencil, the boy had drawn a remarkable representation of an iguana—a smooth, firm outline of the body, with the intricate details of reptilian skin.

'You're very talented. Where did you learn to draw like this?'

'Nowhere. I've just been drawing by myself.'

'Have you made any drawings with paints or charcoal?' Lila pulled some tubes of paint and pieces of charcoal from her canvas bag to demonstrate.

The boy's eyes widened. 'No, I don't have any. Are you a real artist? What's your name?'

Lila laughed softly. 'My name is Lila. I don't know exactly what makes a real artist, but I think I am one, yes.' She was quite charmed by this small boy.

'My name's Carlos and I've never met an artist before.' He hesitated and looked down at his pad. 'Do you think you could show me how to paint?'

Lila's heart melted at the thought that she could help develop the boy's talent, and she quickly assured him that she would be happy to give him some lessons. It sounded as if his parents weren't providing any encouragement, she thought. Maybe it was a large family without much money.

'Tell you what,' she announced happily, 'if you come here on Thursday morning, we can have our first lesson. In the meantime, I'll have to get you some proper supplies.'

He looked up at her, eyes round with excitement. 'I guess it's okay that you scared away the iguana,' he said sheepishly. 'I'm sorry I got mad about it.'

'I'm going to do a little painting now. Would you like to watch?' Lila set up her easel opposite some particularly large and graceful ferns. Somewhat reluctantly, she decided not to put more than a sliver of water at the bottom of the picture. Sunlight on water was difficult to capture, and she didn't intend to spend much time painting in this spot, beautiful as it was. Her real work would be at the ruins.

Lila was delighted at how quietly and intently Carlos observed the progress of her work. He stayed for quite a while, but when Lila decided it was time to pack up her things and return for lunch, she turned and saw that Carlos had slipped away unnoticed while she was absorbed in the scene she was trying to create.

When she got back to the house, she found Françoise basking by the pool in a low-cut bathing suit. '*Ma chérie*, there you are! I hope I have not neglected you. I'm a late sleeper, I'm afraid.'

'I spent a delightful morning, thanks ... Françoise, do you know where I can buy some paints and brushes and things?'

She sat up on her elbows and squinted at Lila. 'You've already used up that whole bag full?'

'Oh no,' Lila laughed softly. 'But this morning I met a boy who would like me to give him some lessons. So far he's been working with only pencil and paper. Probably his parents are poor and can't afford anything else. But he's very talented, and ...'

A goodnatured laugh from Françoise interrupted her. 'My dear, you are too softhearted. You've been here only one day and already you are being Lady Bountiful! But if you are set on it, of course the Peugeot is yours any time. You'll find a variety store on the main street in Merida. They carry some supplies. Tell them you are staying with me ... perhaps they will show you extra consideration. I think they will have what you need.'

The next morning, Lila woke early and hurried downstairs. Rosa was busy brewing the morning coffee.

'Morning, Rosa. I'm going in to Merida this morning. Is there anything you need?' she asked.

'I'll see,' Rosa told her, bustling away to check the cupboards. A few minutes later she was back with a short list of groceries and a straw shopping bag. 'These are some things I can't get in Uxmal, *señorita*. It would be wonderful if you could get them for me.'

'I'd be happy to,' said Lila, thankful for an opportunity to repay some of the kindness that had been shown her.

Lila found the Peugeot easy to handle. It drove like a dream, and she sped along the road to Merida. She passed the civic centre, with its cool, shaded Plaza Mayor, and its twin-towered six-teenth-century cathedral. She found the shops she was looking for without difficulty, although find-ing a place for the Peugeot on the busy streets of downtown Merida wasn't so easy. The traffic was heavy, and the narrow streets were clogged with tourists buying up local treasures to take back home. Lila was on the verge of giving up in frus-tration when she found a spot just big enough to maneouvre into.

After purchasing the items Rosa wanted from a corner grocery store, she found what she thought must be the variety store Françoise had described. By Merida standards, it was incredibly spacious. The display window was filled with a capricious assortment of hardware, household gadgets, stationery, and souvenirs—a kind of one-stop shopping centre for locals and tourists alike.

She found a surprisingly complete stock of painting supplies in the front of the store, next to the window. Consolidating her straw bag and packages in one arm, she intently examined the assortment of acrylic paints. It didn't matter whether she was shopping for herself or someone else, she could spend hours choosing just the right thing.

She was reaching into her bag to pay for her selections when she heard a friendly male voice behind her.

'At least now I don't have to wait for your telephone call!'

Lila turned quickly to find Steve Taylor boyishly grinning down at her. 'What are you doing here?' she asked in surprise.

'I was walking past and happened to look in here. I might have known this would be where I'd find you. I think you've managed to locate the only place on the Yucatan Peninsula that sells paints and brushes.'

'And everything else as well, it looks like,' she laughed.

They left the store together and walked towards the car, stopping every few feet to look at the colourful window displays in the tourist shops which crowded both sides of the main street.

'*Señorita*, come in and try on one of our beautiful handmade peasant dresses.' A dark-skinned woman with a wide smile and sleek back hair tied in a bun was standing in the doorway of her shop. 'Today is special day—very good prices, you will see.'

A suggestion of an aisle had been carved between the tables of pottery and silver jewellery, and the racks of blouses and skirts along the walls. The enthusiasm of the shopkeeper was so infectious that Lila found herself in a curtained alcove trying on a full peasant skirt and matching blouse that had just been made. The light turquoise cotton was bordered in a lace around the neck and elbow-length sleeves, and the layers of the skirt were separated by the same matching lace.

'What did I tell you? It's perfect,' glowed the shopkeeper as Lila emerged. The woman clasped her hands together and looked to Steve for confirmation.

Lila hadn't intended to buy anything for herself since she was on a rather strict budget. But when she saw how the turquoise in the dress accentuated the unusual colour of her eyes, she decided she could somehow make up for the extravagance. Since she was still a little unfamiliar with the foreign currency, she watched while

Steve carried out the firmly entrenched local custom of bargaining. The results seemed to leave everyone satisfied, and they again were on their way. Steve accompanied her to the car, carrying her packages and chatting animatedly about the eccentricities of his latest tour group. Opening the car door for her, he said, 'You know, I'd been kicking myself for letting you go off without a way to contact you. I'm not about to do it again,' he added meaningfully, and she felt her cheeks flush hotly. 'I'd like to take you on that tour I promised you, but I'm busy all this week. How about a week from Monday? I'm off that day.'

Lila hesitated for a moment. Her feelings about getting involved hadn't changed. And she was here to work. Still, Steve was very sweet, and the tour would help her in doing her paintings. Besides, after her encounter with Rafael Blake, Steve offered a welcome contrast. At least he made her feel she was someone special. 'I'd like that,' she said finally. 'Thank you.'

'I like to get an early start. Why don't we meet at eight? Can you be up that early?'

'Oh, sure. See you then.' She watched him waving to her in the rear view mirror as she pulled away.

CHAPTER FOUR

WHEN Thursday morning arrived, Lila woke up to a feeling of anticipation she could not at first trace. She lay in bed briefly, enjoying her feeling of well-being and the thin stripes of morning sun which had found their way through the shutters. Remembering that Carlos' first art lesson would be that morning, she slipped quickly out of bed and walked barefoot across the room to the connecting bathroom.

Enjoying the feel of the thick ivory carpet beneath her feet, Lila marvelled again at the luxury in which she found herself. The money Jonathan had given her for the trip would probably not have covered her expenses, even had she stayed in the least expensive place she could find. Stripping off her nightgown in the pink-tiled bathroom, she gave herself a broad, excited grin in the mirror. Françoise's house was a far cry from the seedy hotel she might have been occupying. Luck was certainly with her on this trip.

Once dressed in khaki slacks and a turquoise tee-shirt, Lila hurriedly gathered up the supplies she had purchased for Carlos and dashed downstairs for a quick breakfast of toast and coffee. Politely refusing Rosa's pleas that she stay and eat a more substantial meal, she hurriedly set off for her meeting with Carlos. When she arrived, the boy was already seated in the spot where she had last seen him, this time busily drawing a fern.

'Hi, Carlos,' said Lila, her eyes twinkling as she looked down at the sturdy boy with his straight dark hair falling into his eyes. 'I brought you something.' She reached into her canvas bag and drew out four tubes of paint and some brushes.

Carlos stared down at his drawing. 'I can't take 'em,' he said, almost in a whisper.

'Can't take them?' she echoed. 'But why ever not?'

'My uncle told me I couldn't,' he said, his eyes still cast downward.

'But why would he do a thing like that?' she demanded incredulously.

'See, my uncle doesn't really like me to draw. He says I have more important things to do with my time. And I know he doesn't like artists. He's afraid I'll start to act the way some artists do. So when I told him that a lady was bringing me some paints, he got very angry and told me I couldn't take them. He said I should know better than to accept gifts from strangers.'

Lila was beginning to burn with anger at the thought that Carlos' talent was being suppressed. It reminded her of her father's attitude towards her own artistic leanings, and the similarity only served to fuel her anger.

'Carlos, will you show me where you live? I'd

like to talk to your uncle.'

'It won't do any good, *señorita*. He's pretty stubborn. He'll just get angry again.'

'I'm willing to give it a try,' she said firmly.

'O.K.,' he said with a sigh. 'But it won't do any good.'

Inwardly, Lila was a little anxious about confronting a strange man about his nephew. Though the boy spoke English very well, she wasn't sure that his uncle would, and she couldn't speak Spanish nearly well enough to argue. Besides, in a way, it wasn't any of her business. She only knew she couldn't stand by and see the boy's talents go to waste.

Lila took Carlos' hand and they set off. After crossing the main road, they took a path that wound through a wooded section on the other side. When they came into a clearing, she saw with a shock that they were headed straight for the estate that belonged to Rafael Blake. She took a deep breath. This certainly wasn't going to make the task any easier! Carlos' uncle must work on the estate. She only hoped they'd be able to find him without running into Mr Blake himself. Lila had no wish to meet him again after the way he had talked to her at the party. He was definitely the most unbearably opinionated and arrogant man she had ever met.

The thought of encountering him here on his own territory made her heart quiver, and the intimidating grandeur of the building added to her fears. The view of the mansion from the road had hardly prepared her for the full impact of its splendour. The heroic scale of the house and its location on the knoll combined to give her an impression of aloof dignity.

Her eyes widened as she approached a magnificent sixteenth-century Elizabethan mansion. The large square-paned windows gave a sense of openness and lightness which balanced the weight of the stone building materials. Green trailing vines with bright yellow flowers grew in the interstices between the windows, adding an element of carefully embroidered detail.

As they ascended the winding brick path, Lila suddenly realised that Carlos planned to take her through the front door. Her pulse quickened at her imprudent decision to confront the boy's uncle. She halted, but Carlos' hand was pulling her forward.

'My uncle usually spends the mornings inside.' He turned the brass knob on the carved mahogany door and they stepped inside. The entryway was cool and dark after the outdoor sunshine. Following closely behind the boy, Lila had time to notice the Indian weavings that hung on the roughly cemented brick walls. Their footsteps on the tile floor echoed loudly in her ears, like the exaggerated ticking of a clock in an otherwise silent space. If Rafael Blake was at home, he could hardly avoid knowing that someone had entered. Thoroughly regretting her impulse to speak to

Carlos' uncle, Lila groped for the words to explain to the boy why she had changed her mind.

A tall brunette clad in a pair of brief shorts and a halter-top appeared in the hall in front of them. 'Were you looking for someone?' she asked coolly.

'Hi, Stephanie,' Carlos answered cheerfully. 'We're going to see my uncle.'

At Carlos' words, Lila recognised the woman Rafael Blake had escorted to the party. Stephanie eyed her with disapproval. 'Who is this, Carlos?'

Lila bristled. Stephanie was acting as if they'd never met. Trembling a little with anger, she answered, 'I'm Lila Fleming. We met at the party on Saturday.' Although she tried to make her voice as cool and even as Stephanie's, it seemed to her to sound soft and a little uncertain.

'Oh, yes.' Stephanie seemed to dismiss her with a flick of her carefully-manicured fingers. 'What do you want with Rafael?'

'Rafael?' Lila gulped at the stunning realisation that Carlos' uncle was Rafael Blake himself. How could she have been so foolish! Her artist's eye should have warned her, since the family resemblance was clear. The man and boy shared the same shining black hair, straight narrow nose, and wide-set dark eyes. If only she had minded her own business, she would never have got into this impossible situation.

The sound of a door opening down the hall set her already quickened pulse racing. Rafael Blake appeared in the doorway, dressed in grey slacks and a short-sleeved sports shirt. 'I'll handle this, Stephanie,' he said brusquely, and Stephanie disappeared with a toss of her hair, leaving Lila and Carlos face to face with Rafael.

'Uncle Rafael,' Carlos announced, 'this is the lady who wants to give me the paints and stuff.'

Rafael Blake's eyes narrowed dangerously. They seemed like fragments of shining onyx in the shadowed hall. Inwardly, Lila cringed and wished she could escape into a nearby mousehole.

'You can run and play, Carlos. I'll speak to Miss Fleming in my study.' Rafael's voice was cold and unfeeling. As Carlos scampered to the front door, Rafael turned abruptly and walked briskly but mechanically back down the hall, leaving Lila to hurry after him. Entering the study, she found him already seated behind a huge, paper-strewn mahogany desk, and she took in the portraits and books which lined the oak-panelled walls before she turned back to Rafael. The chair in front of the desk was already occupied by a sleeping black cat. Reluctant to disloge Rafael's pet without his invitation, Lila ended up standing in front of his desk like a naughty schoolgirl.

She looked down at her dusty slacks and tee-shirt, somehow feeling she would be better equipped to meet the situation if she were more formally dressed. And, she remembered suddenly, biting her lips with vexation, she hadn't even taken the time to put on lipstick that morning. She had barely run a brush through her hair. Rafael Blake, on the other hand, looked as attractive as he had at the party. His sports shirt fitted his broad shoulders and narrow waist so closely, it might have been tailor-made.

'Well?' he challenged.

The little speech Lila had mentally prepared for a poor peasant now seemed so inappropriate that her mind went completely blank. She knew there was no hope of changing the mind of a man who already disapproved of her so strongly. If only she had known that Rafael Blake was Carlos' uncle, she never would have come here.

Rafael began impatiently tapping his fingers on his desk. Breaking the tense silence, he flared, 'By what right do you interfere with me and my nephew?'

Lila gasped with outrage. 'I was not interfering,' she protested. 'I was simply trying to help him.'

'Carlos can get along very well without your help. As can I.' He stood up, apparently intending to dismiss her from his study.

'I offered to help Carlos because I assumed his family was too poor to develop his artistic talents,' Lila retorted furiously, standing her ground. 'Now that I've found out you're his uncle, I know that there's no excuse for neglecting his education.'

'His education, Miss Fleming, is far from being neglected,' Rafael responded through clenched teeth. Although the desk was between them, he seemed to Lila to be towering over her. The muscles in his arms were made clearly visible by his tightened fists. 'I simply will not have him encouraged in worthless pursuits.'

'Art is hardly worthless,' Lila shot back. 'It . . .'

'Indeed?' Rafael's voice dripped with scorn. 'My experience with my brother-in-law taught me that artists can all too easily use their art as an excuse for laziness and frivolity, a reason for neglecting their responsibilities. Carlos will one day have a great deal of money and he will also have the responsibility of managing it wisely. He needs to learn discipline, not licence. Our family has many traditions which I want him to uphold.' Absently, he pushed some papers to the side of his desk.

'Artists care only for themselves and what they call their work. In my experience, they are irresponsible and without morals.'

Lila felt she would choke with fury. 'You are without doubt the most narrow-minded man I've ever known!'

'And you have known many, I am sure.' His dark eyes roved unhurriedly over her silken-skinned features before he sat down again in his chair. He leaned back, and smiled a lazy smile that only served to fan the flame of Lila's anger.

'I'm sure there have been countless men eager to take advantage of a pretty young painter,' he continued. 'It's a pity you've been allowed to take up such a life.' He straightened in his chair. 'I can assure you that will not happen to my nephew.' His voice had developed a knife-sharp edge. 'I forbid you to teach him or buy him gifts. And I forbid you to discuss art or painting with him. I would prefer that he have nothing to do with you, in fact, but he is a stubborn child and he seems to have taken a liking to you. I don't wish to test his obedience too far. But you will be wise to do as I say.'

Lila was shaking with anger. 'How dare you . . .' she began in a high, tight voice, then feared that she was about to burst into tears of rage. Determined not to humiliate herself by allowing him to see her cry, she turned and blindly raced down the hall, hot tears welling in her eyes. As she fumbled with the front door, Stephanie's mocking voice came from behind her.

'Why, Lila! Whatever is the matter?' A glance at Stephanie was all it took to see that the brunette was enjoying her distress. As Lila finally escaped from the house and ran towards the woods, the memory of Stephanie's malicious grin increased her helpless fury.

Back in her room at Françoise's house, Lila felt her tearful rage gradually transform into an icy calm. Never had anyone insulted her so terribly.

How dared he stand there so coolly and collec-
tedly and insinuate that she would corrupt Carlos!
And to insinuate that she was promiscuous! He
was the one with a live-in girl-friend, Lila thought
angrily. She, on the other hand, had never even
had a serious boy-friend.

So why had she just stood there and let him get
away with all the things he had said? She was
furious at him, but more furious at herself. Except
for her father, no man had ever intimidated her so
thoroughly. Of course, she had never known a
man capable of arousing such intense feelings in
her. Inexplicably, she pictured his strongly
muscled arms, so clearly revealed by his thin
sports shirt. What would it be like to be clasped
in such arms? Obviously Rafael Blake was a man
of strong emotions. Would his love be as powerful
as his anger?

She shook her head abruptly, blushing at her
own foolishness. How could she even think such
things about a man who had been so overbearing,
a man who showed no respect for her at all? Lila
buried her face in her hands. The scene with
Rafael had generated a storm of unfamiliar and
contradictory feelings. Restlessly she paced the
length of her room, replaying the argument in
her head. A picture of Rafael standing masterfully behind his desk kept recurring in her
mind, the image as detailed and vivid as a
photograph.

Lila set up her easel on a large section of news-

paper and took out her paints. Obviously she
would have to paint Rafael out of her system. It
was a technique that had always helped her clear
her mind. Hastily she sketched an outline of
Rafael's taut frame leaning forward slightly on
hands braced steadily against the edge of the desk.
Then she began painstakingly mixing colours.
The golden tan of his skin, his gleaming black
hair, the auburn flecks in his dark eyes challenged
her. For some reason she wanted no flaws in this
painting. When she had finished it, she wanted it
to be a perfect representation of Rafael Cornejo
Blake. She was working carefully on shading to
show the outline of his cheekbones when Rosa
spoke softly behind her.

'You did not answer my knocks, *señorita*. I have
come to tell you lunch will be in fifteen minutes
on the veranda.'

'Thank you, Rosa,' Lila murmured, and began
hurriedly cleaning up her paints. In the bathroom
mirror, she noted the traces of tears in her reflec-
tion. With a shrug, she splashed cold water on
her eyes, made a cursory pass through her hair
with her brush, and set off downstairs to find
Françoise.

'Lila,' Françoise announced breathlessly, 'My
boy-friend, Georges, just called to say he will be
arriving today. I will be so happy to see him,' she
glowed. She gestured for Lila to sit down. 'He's
not much to look at, but he's a real man,' she said
with a short laugh.

Lila blushed and looked away as Françoise gave her a wink.

'He adores women and he loves to have a good time. What's more, he's never tried to tie me down. Of all the men I've known since my husband died, he is the most fun.'

'How did you meet him?' Lila asked.

'I met him several weeks ago when he acted as agent for a man I was selling some land to. He was here for a weekend once before, but he says he will stay a little longer this time.'

Lila hesitated. It sounded as if this Georges would be staying in the house. Was Françoise trying to tell her politely that she would need Lila's room for Georges? At her question, Françoise waved a hand as if to dismiss the idea.

'I have plenty of room here. Georges will not be using the guestroom, in any case. You should feel free to stay as long as you like. In fact, I insist that you stay. I'm planning a party for Georges tomorrow night, and of course you must attend.'

'I'll be happy to come to the party,' Lila faltered. The idea of staying with Françoise while Georges was there made her uncomfortable. Still, she wouldn't want to hurt Françoise's feelings after she had been so kind. The best thing would be to locate another place to stay and move out in a day or two, she decided. Françoise would probably be so busy with Georges she would not mind.

'So, what kind of morning did you have?'

Fortunately Lila was saved from answering by

the clickety-clack of the wooden tea cart over the tiles. 'Rosa always spoils me with delicious food,' said Françoise, in mock anger. She unfolded her napkin and draped it over her coral skirt. 'I keep telling her I am getting fat and no one will want me,' she patted her thighs in a demonstration of the seriousness of the situation, 'but she pays no attention.' She gestured with her chin at Lila. 'You are young and slender. You can afford to eat meals like this.'

'Not for more than a few days,' Lila protested. 'I hate to think what would become of my figure if I stayed here for very long!'

Françoise was right about Rosa's cooking, Lila thought, feasting on a Cornish hen grilled with Madeira and cream, saffron rice, and green salad vinaigrette. After a dessert of mangoes sprinkled with lime juice, and more coffee, Françoise announced that she was ready for her afternoon siesta. 'You can see that after a meal such as this, one wants to sleep a little bit. And I try to go along with the local custom. Then I must make myself beautiful and meet Georges at the airport. I'm afraid I'm being a terrible hostess,' she added with an apologetic smile.

'Not at all. I have plenty to keep me busy this afternoon,' Lila was quick to reassure her. 'Please don't worry about me at all.'

Lila lingered for a few minutes on the veranda, savouring the remains of her strong Mexican coffee, and luxuriating in the rich colours and

perfumes surrounding her. A weeping willow at
the corner of the veranda provided shade for a
profusion of pink and white azaleas, and a warm
breeze brought the odour of flowering jasmine.
The beauty of the setting did nothing to dispel a
sudden feeling of loneliness.

She had set out in the morning so cheerful and
full of plans, and Rafael Blake had completely
destroyed her mood. She had few friends in
Uxmal, but it seemed she had at least one enemy.
Two, she corrected herself, remembering
Stephanie's apparent pleasure at her distress. It
seemed particularly sad to feel so upset when she
was surrounded by so much colour and fragrance,
and she stood up abruptly.

Back in her room, she returned immediately to
her painting. She worked intently now, not even
thinking about what she was doing, but allowing
her instincts to take over. Several hours later she
stepped back, wearily brushing her hair from her
face. Knowing she was still too close to the painting to judge it, she carefully cleaned up her paints
and brushes. Then, for the first time since her
arrival, she pulled back the shutters to see the
garden overlooked by her windows.

The riot of colour that greeted her eyes was as
refreshing as a dip in the ocean. Cascading down
terraced hillsides between pink and white oleanders were vines of purple bougainvillaea. Stone
steps nestled into the hillside and found their way to
a gravel path, which intersected the bright green

lawn. Bordering the lawn on the far side were splashes of purple and yellow perennials. An age-old stone wall covered with wisteria and pale pink climbing roses provided a border between the garden and the swimming pool farther down. A small thatched cabaña with bamboo chairs and lounges stood at the opposite side of the pool, where she caught sight of Françoise and a slightly portly man. Their sudden embrace caused Lila to draw back from the window with embarrassment. So Georges had arrived!

Lila felt like an intruder. At least she could give them some time alone by having dinner in her room, she thought, and she slipped down to the kitchen to tell Rosa. Her dinner arranged, she allowed herself a critical appraisal of her painting of Rafael. She had to admit, it was by far the best portrait she had ever done. And it was astonishing that she had been able to do it all from memory. Rafael's aristocratic face stared at her coolly from across the room. His lips were compressed in anger and disapproval, his posture was tense and slightly threatening. Without conscious thought, Lila had dressed him as a seventeenth-century nobleman rather than in modern clothes. The rich clothing suited him, she decided. She would have to make some decisions about the background, but she had done enough for one day.

Now that she felt somewhat more relaxed, she allowed her mind to drift back to her meeting with Rafael. Was it possible he really believed the things he had implied about her? She had never experienced such contemptuous disapproval from anyone. Even her father, as much as he disapproved of artists, had never hinted that she had loose morals or that she lacked character. It was almost impossible to defend herself against the variety of accusations Rafael had made against her. Instead, after each meeting with him, she was left with the nagging feeling that she had stood helplessly by while he maligned her to his heart's content. The thing to do, she decided, was to put Rafael Blake firmly out of her mind. Since there was no need to see him again, there was also no need to worry about his opinion of her.

She held firmly to her resolution for the rest of the evening. But when she fell asleep, her dreams revolved around a tall, black-haired man. In the first dream, he lectured her angrily, his voice growing insistently louder and more accusatory. When Lila tried to answer his charges she found she had lost her voice and could only weep silently. In the second dream, the same man held her in a passionate embrace which left her knees weak with desire. Then suddenly he abandoned her to pursue a scantily clad brunette, while Lila ran frantically after him. She awoke with only a dim awareness of her dreams, but she knew the night's sleep had left her exhausted and bewildered.

Her first meeting with Georges did nothing to soothe her. Françoise's boy-friend was a rather

short, unattractive man with sand-coloured hair.
He was breakfasting alone when Lila appeared in
the dining room, and made an elaborate show of
leaping to his feet and pulling out a chair for her.

'Ah, you must be Françoise's lovely young
house guest.'

'Yes, I'm Lila,' she responded neutrally.

'I'll bet that's short for Delilah, isn't it?'
Georges continued with a suggestive smile.

'No, my name's just Lila.' Where was
Françoise? she wondered, looking around nervously. Georges was making her quite uncomfortable. He took every opportunity during
their conversation to survey her figure and his
eyes returned frequently to her breasts, which
were faintly outlined by her thin blue blouse.

'I hope we will become better acquainted.' His
hand on her bare forearm made Lila jump nervously in her chair. Hastily finishing her coffee,
she excused herself abruptly and escaped to her
room. Lila shuddered at the memory of his touch.
How could Françoise like such a man? To ensure
that she would not see Georges again before
Françoise was up, she crept out the front door
with her bag of paints and brushes in search of a
secluded spot.

Lunch on the veranda with Georges and
Françoise turned out to be only slightly more
comfortable than breakfast. Françoise was animatedly describing the difficulties of arranging a
party at the last minute. 'I have spent the entire

morning on the telephone. There will be no siesta for *me* today; there's still so much to arrange.' She paused as if suddenly remembering her two house guests. 'Georges, you and Lila will have to amuse yourselves this afternoon, I'm afraid.'

Georges smiled meaningfully at Lila, while she did her best to ignore him politely. Although he was very attentive to Françoise during the meal, Lila several times had the sense that his knee brushed against hers under the table, and she irritably moved away. The situation would have to be tolerated until she could leave without hurting Françoise, Lila told herself. To avoid Georges, she decided to spend the afternoon in her room working on her portrait of Rafael. She would have preferred to allow more time to elapse before adding the background and final touches, but there seemed little choice.

Her work occupied her until it was time to shower and change for the party. She spent a long time basking in a steaming hot shower, hoping it would relax her. The day's incidents with Georges had left her tense and irritable. Furthermore, she had the recurring thought that Rafael might be at this party, just as he had been at the last one. Although both Rafael and Françoise had made it quite clear that they did not mix socially except in very unusual circumstances, Lila could not banish a feeling of tingling excitement and apprehension. It was almost as if she wanted to see Rafael again, she thought in some bewilderment.

And the thought of another encounter with him was far from restful.

After a quick survey of her wardrobe, she decided to wear her white A-line dress to the party. Once she left Françoise's house, there would probably be no more parties. Since she had worn the yellow dress to the last party, she might as well wear her only other dress on this occasion. As an added incentive, the square neck was rather modest and might even serve to discourage Goerges.

After a light application of lipstick and mascara, Lila examined herself in the mirror. To her own eyes, she appeared young and unsophisticated. What did Rafael see that caused him to hurl such insults at her? And what did Georges see that led him to think his advances would be acceptable? Lila shrugged and reluctantly turned to join the guests who were now beginning to arrive.

CHAPTER FIVE

As soon as she stepped into the living room, Lila was aware that this party was very different from the one she had first attended in Uxmal. The women seemed more heavily made up, and there was considerably more drinking. By the second hour, the cigarette smoke was so thick that Lila's eyes were burning. The music from a small combo was making her head throb.

She wandered out away from the house to escape the noise and smoke. This was a side of the grounds she hadn't been on before. She didn't know how far Françoise's property extended, but about the time she could hear only faint strains of the music, she found an old stone bench and sat down gratefully. The monotonous sound of cicadas rubbing their wings together came as a relief after the din of the party. As Lila drew deep breaths of the warm night air, pleasantly scented with jasmine, she heard footsteps approaching from the direction she had just come. Her dismay when Georges suddenly appeared around the trunk of a palm tree was so strong that it must have been plainly written on her face. Georges' glowing cigarette cast eerie shadows on his face as he inhaled, giving him a malevolent look. He tossed the cigarette to the ground and sat down clumsily beside her. Lila realised that he had had too much to drink and her mind began racing to invent an excuse to escape.

'I was just on my way back to the party, Georges. Coming with me?' As she attempted to stand up, Georges' moist hand pressed down heavily on her shoulder. Annoyed, Lila moved sideways to free herself and found that she was caught suddenly in a whisky-scented embrace. 'Stop it, Georges. Stop it!' she ordered furiously, only to feel his arms tighten.

Georges placed his mouth on her silken cheek, mumbling entreaties and endearments. Filled with distaste and horror, she struggled in his grip. Her panic mounted as she realised that she couldn't free herself. At the touch of Georges' mouth on hers, she wrenched her head away. Undaunted, he continued his lovemaking, pausing only to mutter, 'No need to make a scene, Delilah.'

He was now tearing at the buttons at the neck-line of her dress. Lila tried ineffectually to push him away, digging the heels of her hands into his chest and pressing with all her strength. Realising that he was overpowering her, she finally screamed, 'Let me go!' As her back was pressed against the bench, two masculine hands gripped Georges' shoulders and pulled him away from her. Lila's heart skipped violently when she recognised her rescuer as Rafael Blake. She sat frozen with embarrassment as Rafael lectured a sullen, speechless Georges and sent him back to the party.

As Rafael turned his attention to her, Lila bit her lip. She could not imagine anything more humiliating than to be found in such a situation by him. He had already made it clear that he considered her promiscuous, and this scene wasn't likely to improve his opinion of her. Each time she encountered him, she was at a disadvantage. She cringed inside to think that even though he had been consistently disapproving of her, she owed him some gratitude for rescuing her from Georges. She would have to acknowledge that she was in his debt. 'Thank you for your help,' she murmured, raising her eyes shyly to meet his gaze.

'My pleasure,' Rafael drawled, his lips curling slightly at the corners. 'I'm always glad to be of help to attractive young women, even when they bring their troubles on themselves.'

Lila dropped her eyes quickly to hide the effect of his words. She had known he would put the worst possible interpretation on the episode, but it was still painful to hear him suggest that she was to blame.

'You can't be completely unaware of the effect you have on men,' he continued, 'but since you apparently didn't enjoy being attacked by a drunk, maybe you should think twice next time before you turn on the charm.'

His assumption that she had led Georges on was painful, but she had expected something of the sort. Determined not to let him know how easily he could hurt her, she shot back, 'Yes, I made a mistake with Georges. Most of the men I flirt with are more refined!'

She could see by the sudden flash in his eyes that her reckless remark had changed his mood from icy disapproval to rage. He gripped her shoulders painfully and pulled her to her feet. 'You can be shameless when you want to be, can't you?' he said harshly.

Lila forced herself not to flinch, although his fingers seemed to be burning into her flesh. She looked directly up into his face, which seemed uncomfortably close to hers. 'You've said all along that I was immoral, so my shamelessness shouldn't come as any surprise to you.' Unable to bear his closeness any longer, she twisted angrily away from his grip.

'I suppose you're right,' he spat back contemptuously. 'Your behaviour has been true to form. For some reason, even knowing what I did about you, I still expected something better. Perhaps I was deceived by your innocent appearance.'

For a moment, Lila was tempted to drop the pretence that she had behaved badly and admit that Georges had come upon her unexpectedly, but her hope that she could correct his impression of her was dispelled by the sneer that came to his lips as he glanced at the torn neckline of her dress. She reached up quickly to hold the dress together as Rafael picked up the button Georges had ripped off and handed it to her with an exaggerated bow.

'Another memento of your life-style,' he gibed.

Lila's temper flared. 'I don't know why you even bothered to help me, since you're so sure I'm entirely to blame for all this. After all, it's not as if you were protecting my honour.'

'No,' Rafael agreed coolly, 'I was protecting my own: I could never ignore anyone's cries for help, even if the person in trouble is the one who caused the situation in the first place.'

Lila shrugged. She had no wish to extend the battle, no matter how much Rafael insulted her. It was clear she would never change his opinion of her, so why should she bother to argue? 'I think it's time I went back to the house,' she said resignedly.

Rafael nodded, his face suddenly sombre in the moonlight. 'Yes, I'm sure someone has missed you by now.'

Lila looked at him silently for a moment. When his expression did not lighten, she turned and set off for Françoise's house as quickly as the dark would allow. She was very aware of his eyes following her, and held herself stiffly until she was sure his view of her was blocked by some trees.

To avoid being seen by anyone else in her dishevelled state, she slipped into the house through the kitchen. Miraculously, Rosa was not there, and she was able to creep upstairs unnoticed. She approached the door to her room with relief. Her knees were beginning to tremble slightly. The events of the evening had upset and exhausted her and all she wanted to do was fall into bed. First thing in the morning she would find a hotel room somewhere and move out.

With fingers made clumsy by the fright she had experienced, she unzipped her dress and removed the rest of her clothes, then began crossing the room to her wardrobe for her nightgown. As she passed the door she heard a faint sound of metal clicking against metal, and whirling around to face the door, she saw the handle jiggling back and forth. She was suddenly terrifyingly aware of her nakedness, and the knowledge that the door was locked did little to slow her racing pulse. Swiftly she snatched up her dress from the floor and clutched it to her breasts, trying to cover herself.

She stood frozen in this position for what seemed like hours, long after the doorhandle was still and footsteps had retreated slowly down the hall. Logically, she told herself it could have been any one of the guests at the party. There was enough drinking going on to account for almost anything, but the events of the evening convinced her it was Georges, and she knew she could not spend another night under the same roof with him.

Trembling violently, she pulled on a pair of slacks and a shirt, then gathered the rest of her clothes together and stuffed them haphazardly into her suitcase. After assembling her art supplies and stuffing them into her canvas bag, she paused to inspect her portrait of Rafael. His dark, arrogant eyes returned her gaze, serving only to entangle further her complex web of emotions. She brushed the painting with her finger to see that it was dry enough to take, then took a large piece of muslin from her canvas bag and wrapped it securely. After a quick survey of the room to see that she had everything, she took paper and a pen from her purse and tried to compose a note to Françoise.

Tears came to her eyes as she tried to think of what she could say. Disappearing into the middle of the night was a fine way to repay her hospitality! But Lila felt she had no choice. With a helpless shrug, she scribbled a note and propped it in front of the dressing-table mirror, picked up her bags, and turned to walk out of the door.

Her silent trip back through the kitchen was uneventful, but fear of another encounter with Georges left her mouth dry and her heart hammering.

She had no idea where she would spend the night, but she resolved to keep looking until she found a room. Despite Françoise's assertion that every hotel was full, there must be a vacancy somewhere, perhaps in a less desirable place. Lila thought nothing could be more unpleasant than the situation she was escaping. Shifting her cargo in her hands, she began her eerie walk into town.

Though she had little more baggage than when she first arrived, it now felt like leaden weights dangling from the ends of her arms. A bruise was developing at the spot where the canvas of the portrait rubbed against her arm, and by the time she had covered half a mile she was stopping every few feet to stretch her fingers and readjust her bags. As tears of frustration stung her eyes, she stumbled to the side of the road and sank down on to her suitcase.

As unpleasant as this was, it was still better than staying in the same house with Georges. Somehow, she had to try to make it the rest of the way. She guessed that she must have at least a mile left to cover before she reached the town, and her courage nearly failed her. Heaving a deep sigh, she stood and tried to pick up her bags again, but her hands were too tired to grip properly and the bags dropped heavily to the ground. Lila fell back on her suitcase and buried her face in her hands.

'Let me guess,' a familiar voice began, and she threw back her head in alarm to find Rafael towering above her, a sardonic smile spreading across his face. 'Someone else took you up on one of your provocative invitations, and you got more than you bargained for. Is that it?' he drawled.

How could he be so cruel in the face of her obvious misery? Other than being a painter, she hadn't done anything to deserve these attacks on her virtue.

'Or are you just on the prowl?' he continued mercilessly.

'Well, if I were, I certainly wouldn't be looking for you!' she shot back.

'Just what are you doing out in the road in the middle of the night, if I may ask?'

Lila looked down and let out a dismal sigh. 'I have to find a place to stay. I . . . I can't stay with Françoise any more.' A sob ended her sentence as the images of the evening returned.

'So you did get more than you bargained for,' Rafael concluded. His tone indicated that he was confident of having assessed the situation correctly. 'Maybe it's time you learned not to create desires you don't want to fulfil. Or did you just have a last-minute change of heart?' His narrowed eyes raked over her, and Lila clenched her teeth in anger. She couldn't believe that he would continue to taunt her this way. She drew a deep breath before raising her eyes to meet his. Her voice full of rebellion, she said, 'What business is it of yours anyway, whom I choose to encourage? I'm not aware that you have any claim on me.'

Rafael stared down into her eyes, his gaze penetrating her being. 'No, and even if I did, I doubt it would do me much good in controlling your provocative behaviour. I'm concerned merely because you appear to be incapable of looking after yourself,' Rafael continued, taking her chin in his hand. 'Apparently it's necessary to remind you that this is the second time tonight you've needed my help. I can hardly venture out of my house without being called upon to rescue you from your own stupidity.' Lila turned her head away from his towering presence. Now, apparently, he not only thought she was lacking in virtue, she was also stupid! As much as she rebelled inside, she was too weak to defend herself further.

Rafael took her wrists in his hands and drew her up. 'Come with me,' he ordered. Lila complied, her legs now barely able to support her. Her weariness was the only thing that made it possible to submit to his dominance. She allowed him to take both of her bags, reserving the wrapped portrait for herself, and stumbled down the road after him.

She followed him in silence for several minutes, their footsteps punctuated by the occasional cry of a night bird. 'What brought you out so late at night?'

Rafael shrugged. 'I couldn't sleep. I thought a walk would relax me.' He shot her a glance that seemed full of hidden meaning and smiled lazily. 'Maybe I sensed you were in trouble again.'

Lila looked away, confused by the change in his mood. His smile had erased all her anger, and she found herself hoping again that she could somehow gain his approval.

'What would your mother say if she knew how recklessly you were behaving here?' Rafael went on, shattering her momentary illusion of peace. He began ticking off her sins on his fingers. 'First, you accept the invitation of a woman you know nothing about, and move into her house like the fly in the spider's parlour.'

Lila bridled at Rafael's analogy, but he ignored her reaction to continue his lecture. 'Then you find yourself in deep water when you flirt with an unprincipled drunkard who's nearly old enough to be your father. Then, just to make your adventures complete, you wander around the roads in the middle of the night as if you were perfectly capable of defending yourself. Your parents wouldn't have a moment's peace if they knew what you were doing.'

'In the first place,' Lila responded with as much heat as she could muster through her exhaustion, 'there's just my father, and I doubt he'd be interested. In the second place,' she added with heavy sarcasm, 'why should I worry, since you seem to have appointed yourself my guardian?'

'Is your father a widower?' Rafael enquired with what she considered unusual tact.

'Yes,' she answered simply. 'My mother died last year.'

'I'm sorry,' Rafael replied softly. 'Was your parents' marriage a happy one?'

'Probably,' Lila replied thoughtfully, 'but it's not the kind of marriage I want.'

'So,' Rafael remarked sardonically, 'you have ideas on marriage. I will defer to your vast experience. How do you view the perfect marriage?'

'Well,' she said slowly, not sure she was ready to reveal herself to him, 'I want a marriage based on love. I mean real love, for the life of the marriage, not just habit or loneliness or a feeling of obligation. I want my husband to be at home sometimes,' she went on, her tiredness making her voluble, 'not always busy at work. I want to care for him in a way that I've never cared for anyone, and I want him to feel the same way about me.'

'Candlelight dinners and frilly nightgowns,' said Rafael, looking down at her with a supercilious smile. 'Is that what you're talking about?'

'Well, what would be wrong with that?' Lila countered. 'Anyway, I'm really trying to describe something much deeper.'

'No doubt,' he said cynically. 'But you're not likely to find that here on earth.'

'Well, if I can't have the kind of marriage I want, then I'd just as well do without it,' she replied, a little angered by his attitude.

'Yes, you seem to be able to find ways of satisfying your needs without benefit of the form of marriage.'

'Where are you taking me?' Lila asked, deciding her best course was to ignore his remarks. She was growing increasingly tired and wondered how much farther her legs would agree to carry her.

He looked at her with one eyebrow raised. 'To Palmera House. You'll never get into a hotel at this hour, and anyway, I am appointing myself

your chaperone. Without one, I'm afraid your
recklessness will lead to serious trouble, either for
you or for someone else. Besides, it's easier this
way. It will save me the trouble of rescuing you
every ten minutes.'

Lila desperately wanted a bed, and the thought
of staying in Rafael's house was somehow exciting. Still, she couldn't just agree to go home with
him without making it clear that she had no in-
tention of letting him dominate her. 'I'm perfectly
capable of taking care of myself,' she said softly
as they approached his front door. 'Whatever you
may think, I don't need protection.'

Rafael was silent as he unlocked the door.
'Perhaps not,' he remarked finally, seeming very
pensive. He touched her shoulder lightly to guide
her towards a dark oak stairway, and her skin
tingled at the contact of his fingers. A shiver of
anticipation ran through her as they climbed the
stairs.

To the left of the stairs, Rafael opened the door
on to a spacious, sparsely furnished bedroom and
put her bags inside the door. He stood silently in
the doorway for a few moments, the muted light
from the bedroom outlining his sharp, masculine
features. He looked down, studying her face, and
her heart began thudding inside, as she con-
sciously focused her eyes on his chest, unable to
meet his probing gaze. She recognised now that
this man had a disconcerting power over her, but
only part of her wanted to escape. She stood

motionless, hypnotised by his nearness.

He took her chin in his hands, slowly tilting it upward. 'I don't know why I should worry about you—you don't seem to be concerned. But I do,' he said. The warm breath of his words fell in light, intimate footsteps on her cheeks. 'And you can't deny you have a certain knack for foolishness.' Slowly he lowered his mouth, his lips pressing against hers with an overpowering mixture of tenderness and authority. As she felt the length of him press against her, her breath was completely taken away, and she was powerless to resist. He was arousing her senses beyond anything in her experience. The blood began throbbing in her lips as he sought out and excited each nerve ending. Involuntarily, she twined her arms around his neck, searching for an anchor in the sea of sensuality he was creating for her.

He pulled away then, leaving her trembling and shaken with the awareness of his effect on her. She averted her eyes in an attempt to mask her vulnerability. She could not bear for him to realise he held a special power over her.

'I'll leave a note for the housekeeper to tell her you're here,' he said huskily. 'I don't want to wake her at this hour.'

Lila eyed his dark frame as he retreated down the hall. She had never known a man like Rafael Blake before. He was a disconcerting mixture of fire and ice, at times filled with tender passion, and at other times as unfeeling as iron. Maybe it was the mixture of Spanish and English in him, but she had no idea what to expect from him.

Her limbs aching, she piled her clothes on a heavy, carved wooden chair. Before turning off the small reading lamp next to the bed, she looked around the room, mentally comparing it to the one she had left earlier that night. It was not only that Rafael's guestroom was masculine while Françoise's was determinedly feminine. It was also that this room gave her a sense of permanence and solidity. The tall, heavy wardrobe next to the closet seemed to have stood there for at least a century. The colourful weavings which decorated the grey stone walls were in traditional patterns and could easily have been acquired generations ago. Lila sighed as she clicked off the light and sank back on to the pillows. Despite the conflicting emotions Rafael aroused in her, it was comforting to be—at least temporarily—in a place where she felt protected.

CHAPTER SIX

FOR a few moments after she opened her eyes the next morning, Lila didn't know where she was or how she had come there. She began reconstructing the events of the night before, as she watched the pattern of leaves on the curtains made by the sun shining through the trees. And then it all came back. Her aching shoulders and sore hands recalled her exertions, and she grimaced as she realized that Françoise would just now be finding the note she had left. She turned over and buried her face in her pillow. Her embarrassment at leaving Françoise's house so suddenly was momentarily enough to tempt her to hide from the world by staying in bed all day.

But no, there was no way she could continue to stay in this house. For one thing, she didn't know how to face Rafael again after her uninhibited response to him the night before. It was painfully clear that the kiss could have meant nothing to him. But, she realised suddenly, since he seemed to think she was quite indiscriminate, he would most likely assume that their kiss was equally unimportant to her. As long as she was able to hide the fact that his effect on her was unusually powerful, she need not be afraid of making a fool of herself.

The house seemed strangely quiet for mid-morning, she noted. Surely Rafael, Stephanie, and Carlos wouldn't all be sleeping late. Somehow Lila had forgotten Stephanie last night. Certainly with her around there wouldn't be a repetition of last night's kiss.

In any case, it would be best to leave. The idea of Rafael setting himself up as her chaperone was insane, and it could only lead to further battles with him. Perhaps he was right in thinking she needed protection, but if so, it was Rafael himself she needed protection from. 'Ridiculous!' she said aloud, and sat up suddenly in bed. She was perfectly capable of taking care of herself under any circumstances.

Rafael's housekeeper, Maria, turned out to be a bird-like elderly lady who immediately took Lila in hand when she went downstairs. She insisted on cooking her a sumptuous breakfast of blueberry muffins, poached eggs, and sausage, served on patterned blue and white bone china.

'When you're finished, you must let me give you a tour of the house. Mr Blake tells me you'll be here for a while, so you may as well know your way around.'

Lila was annoyed at Rafael's presumption that she was going to stay. Maybe because she had let him kiss her he imagined that she was completely under his thumb!

To set the record straight, she said, 'Maria, I'm going to be leaving today to stay in a hotel. It was too late last night, that's the only reason I'm here. After all,' she added, trying to sound sincere, 'I certainly wouldn't want to impose on Mr Blake.'

'Oh, I'm sure you wouldn't be imposing,' Maria replied. 'I thought Mr Blake was sure you were staying. But you must do what you want,' she added, as Lila shook her head vehemently. She poured more coffee into Lila's cup. 'Would you like me to call and try to make a reservation for you? It is often difficult to find a place to stay here.'

Lila agreed gratefully, and Maria disappeared down the hall, only to return a few minutes later with the report that there were three tour groups in town which had taken up all the available rooms. 'There won't be any vacancies for at least four days,' she said apologetically as Lila grimaced in disappointment. From what Françoise had said, she should have known the hotels would still be full. 'Still, you'll be comfortable here. And Mr Blake has his mind made up that you're staying. Once he makes his mind up, it's pretty hard to change it.'

I can certainly believe that! Lila murmured secretly into her coffee.

She was intrigued by the idea of seeing the rest of the house. She could find her way to her bedroom, the dining room, and the study, but the layout of the house and the various rooms that opened off the long hallways remained a mystery. But not for long. Maria seemed intent on showing Lila practically every corner of the great mansion and describing the details of its history.

With some dread, Lila expected to run into Stephanie during their tour. But Maria quickly removed her fears in part of the running commentary which accompanied their walk. Stephanie had apparently returned home. 'She received a long-distance telephone call, and then left in a big hurry,' she said, shrugging her tiny shoulders.

'The west wing here wasn't part of the original house,' Maria continued. 'Christopher Blake—the grandfather—added on to the original house when his son married and brought his wife here to raise their family.' She gave a long sigh as she closed the door to one of the unused bedrooms. 'With Rafael being a bachelor, I'm afraid this wing doesn't get much use these days. The size of the house fairly begs for a family again,' she complained, shaking her head slowly.

Downstairs too, they went from room to room, often up or down a step or two, beneath low lintels back to the hall, with its foot-square oak beams and highly polished stone floor. 'I've saved the most delightful treasures for last,' Maria whispered with suppressed glee, as she opened the door to Rafael's study.

When Lila saw the large mahogany desk, the memory of her last visit to this room came rushing back to her. The room was as imbued with Rafael's presence as if he were standing behind the desk right now.

'These are Mr Blake's forebears,' Maria told her, indicating the array of family portraits which lined the south wall.

Lila read the gold name plates beneath each. Rafael's father had been a noble-looking gentleman with Rafael's firm chin and finely chiselled features. It was easy to tell that Rafael's mother had once been quite beautiful, and a trace of coquetry was discernible in her smile. But it was the grandfather that really arrested her eyes. She didn't know if it was his commanding pose, or the severity of his head, but she sensed something kingly in his character, as if he were well aware of his greatness.

'Christopher Blake,' Lila read the name half aloud as Maria stood at her elbow nodding. 'How did he happen to end up here in the Yucatan, Maria?'

'Oh, it's a fascinating story. You see, Christopher Blake was the younger of two sons. According to English law, the firstborn son was to receive all the father's inheritance, so the second son would have had very little. Well, Christopher apparently wasn't going to settle back and take second place.' Maria leaned towards Lila as if about to let her in on a secret, 'Rafael takes after him in that respect, to be sure.'

'Well, he went first to South America and struck it big in silver there. A little later, he began importing and exporting all sorts of precious metals between here and England. And when he took his Spanish bride, he built this house for her. She was a famous beauty, they say, and could have had her pick of men. Her family was not in favour of her marrying an Englishman, so she ran off with Christopher Blake when she was supposed to be at her aunt's house. It was quite a scandal at the time. Of course, Mr Blake travelled all over the world, but this has been the family home ever since.'

'And he picked up all the paintings and sculpture we saw during his travels?' Lila was still a little stunned by all she'd seen that morning.

'Many of them, yes. His wife had a hand in most of the selections. She had an appreciation for beautiful things. But you haven't seen the most beautiful one of all,' Maria said, laying a hand on her arm. She looked around to assure herself that they were alone, then tiptoed over to the sideboard on the opposite wall. Over the drawers hung a medieval sword. The upper portion of the long tapering blade was incised with arabesques, and inset into the pommel were four carnelian stones.

From the underside of a right-hand drawer, Maria produced a small key, which she then used to unlock the centre cabinet. She withdrew a velvet pouch and came over to Lila to place the contents in her hand.

Lila's eyes all but popped out of her head. It was a gold brooch, in the Renaissance style, set with pearls around the lower edges, and showing two enamelled lovers holding hands amidst gold foliage and flowers. Between the lovers' heads was an oval-shaped diamond, and beneath that a cabochon ruby.

'Did this belong to Christopher Blake?' Lila asked in a whisper.

'Yes, it did. And there's a tradition attached to it. Each of the Blakes has given it to the woman he married . . . that is up until Rafael's generation. He may break the tradition by remaining a bachelor.'

'Oh, I don't think so, Maria. After all, there's Stephanie.' Lila thought she detected a slight wrinkling of Maria's nose, but she couldn't be sure.

'Anything is possible, I suppose. Goodness knows, he could have his pick of the ladies, but . . .'

The sound of the front doorbell sent Maria scurrying to replace the jewel. 'I'll have to answer the door,' she said as she hurried out of the study. 'Lunch will be at noon in the dining room. You'll be eating by yourself today, I'm afraid. Rafael and Carlos are away doing errands.'

'Okay,' Lila called after Maria's rapidly retreating back. 'Thank you for showing me everything.'

After lunch, Lila returned to her room to settle in. She opened the bedroom closet to hang up her things and her stomach churned nervously when she noticed several of Stephanie's dresses still inside. That seemed to leave no doubt that Stephanie was returning—it was just a question of when. Alongside the cerise dress and the white jump suit were several very expensive-looking cocktail dresses, and a light blue peignoir with fur around the sleeves. She was relieved Stephanie wasn't in the house now, but her clothes would serve as a disquieting reminder. She pushed Stephanie's clothes to one side and hung up her own.

Carefully she unwrapped her portrait of Rafael and placed it on the long double dressing table. She stepped back across the room to study it critically. As little as she understood the man, she had somehow managed to capture him perfectly on canvas. With a sense of satisfaction, she placed it at the back of the closet. She didn't want Maria to find it, since she would undoubtedly tell Rafael.

The next day was to be her tour of the ruins with Steve. He had made a big point, she thought with an amused smile, of wanting to start the tour very early in the morning. That was the way the official tours were set up, so that people could be back indoors before the real heat of the day began. So, after supper, Lila took out her white slacks and low-heeled sandals and set them on the bed. After laying out two or three of her blouses alongside the slacks for comparison, she selected the tangerine one, with cap sleeves and round neck. She added her notebook and handbag to the morning pile, and crawled into bed.

At breakfast, the house seemed totally silent, except for the kitchen sounds Maria was making in preparing the day's meals. Lila had no idea whether or not Rafael and Carlos were at home. It hardly mattered, since all during breakfast she was preoccupied with the idea of the tour. She could hardly wait to start her painting of the ruins, and the tour should make her feel ready to dive into her work. She was hoping Steve would be able to give her a feel for the Mayan culture, which seemed so full of mystery.

As she approached the ruins, she could discern the tops of the temples which broke from the sea of green jungle. She spotted Steve in a small crowd of tourists gathered around the entrance. His hair was bleaching to almost white in the sun. When he caught sight of Lila, his blue eyes smiled radiantly, and he came towards her in a long-legged boyish stride.

'Wow!' He glowed with admiration as he took in the picture of her. 'Just everyday luck in the life of a tour guide, I guess,' he smiled. 'Where have you been? I suppose you think the ruins aren't going to crumble if you're a few minutes late,' he teased.

'If I'd arrived much earlier, we would have needed a flashlight for the tour,' she quipped.

'You have a great treat in store for you,' Steve promised, as he led her towards the towering out-

croppings of white limestone. 'Let's take a look at
the Palace of the Governors first. As I'm a bud-
ding architect, this one holds a special fascination
for me.'

It was a long, low building, plain below the
cornice, and ornamented with all sorts of elaborate, if enigmatic, sculptures which formed a sort
of arabesque. The building had a powerful
impact, in its sheer immensity. Steve, in a demonstration of the perfection of its construction,
showed her how the thousands of joints made
by the façade's finely cut stones were almost
totally imperceptible. The grandest ornament was
a carved serpent over the centre doorway. Around
the head of the serpent were rows of hierogly-
phics, perhaps a record of the Mayans' work in
constructing the building.

They escaped from the dazzling sunshine into
the cool black chambers of the interior. The
cement floors were still hard in some places, but
where they had endured long exposure to the sun,
Lila could feel the cement crumbling under her
thin sandals. At almost every step, tenant swallows zoomed out in a frenzy. Steve was in his
glory, explaining to Lila all the architectural details of the walls, ceilings, and support beams.

From the Palace of the Governors, they
wandered among a growing throng of tourists
towards Uxmal's large, unrestored Ball Court.
Towering walls flanked a long, narrow court, now
carpeted by millions of yellow and white wild-

flowers. It was here, more than five hundred years ago, that the great sporting spectacles were played out. Lila could almost hear the cheering and shouting of the spectators echoing back and forth between the walls. Steve shaded his eyes and pointed up to the ledge underneath the top of the walls, where hundreds of swallows were nesting.

A short walk across a broad plaza brought them to a grouping of four structures arranged in a quadrangle around a central courtyard.

'What's this one called, Steve?'

'It's called the Nunnery, but don't ask me why,' he said, shrugging his shoulders. 'For some reason, the Spanish named it that.'

The exterior of each group of buildings was a dead wall, with no doors to the outside. Each was ornamented with the same rich, elaborately carved designs Lila had noticed on the other structures. Sections of diamond latticework design—one of the oldest Mayan motifs—alternated with slabs of unadorned stone. They stood for a while within the courtyard examining the surrounding compartments, and concluded that the Mayans had masterfully designed the four façades to have the utmost variety as well as harmony. All of the façades had originally been painted, and traces of red were still visible in the crevices.

The high point of the morning for Lila was the Temple of the Dwarf—a pyramid that enclosed numerous buried temples, and was topped by one that began a hundred and twenty-five feet above the ground. Steve took hold of her arm and tried to keep Lila from looking down, as they scaled the high steps which rose at a dizzying forty-five-degree angle to the small House of the Dwarf on top. Cameras were snapping all around as tourists perched on their steps and tried to capture the height of the temple in their photos.

Once they had arrived at the top, all her dizziness vanished, and they were treated to a cool breeze and unequalled view of the surrounding jungle. She could see that for every excavated temple, there were a half dozen more—overgrown, alluring mounds of mysterious rubble. Casting her gaze beyond these mounds brought a thudding recognition. The perch on top of this pyramid offered a clear view of Palmera House. She had just been silently congratulating herself for managing to banish Rafael Blake from her thoughts all morning. Now this intrusion suddenly wiped out that small victory. She closed her eyes, trying to redirect her thoughts.

'Why is this one called the Temple of the Dwarf?' As the words left her lips, she caught sight of a small statue of a dwarf on the temple wall. 'Maybe it has something to do with that statue over there,' she said, cocking her head towards it.

Steve looked towards the sculpture. 'It has something to do with a Mayan legend of some kind,' he answered vaguely. 'But I'm going to turn into a dwarf if we don't go and have something to eat,' he laughed. 'How about letting me treat you to some lunch?'

The moment he mentioned it, she realised she had worked up a terrific appetite. She'd been so engrossed in the ruins, she was completely oblivious to the recent complaints from her stomach. 'That sounds wonderful. I guess I am a little hungry.'

The path to the restaurant—a large, open affair with a thatched roof—was lined with local peddlers thrusting souvenirs into the afternoon sun. Steve urged Lila on, saying, 'Don't look at any of the souvenirs or we'll be surrounded and we'll never get to lunch.'

Despite his protests, Lila paused to examine some packets of postcards and finger some small replicas of the ruins. After all, she reasoned, why shouldn't she have a souvenir of her trip? Steve laughed at her reasoning. 'You have your new dress, and you'll have your paintings to remind you of the ruins.'

Lila had to admit the strength of his argument. Still, it didn't seem right to go on a trip without at least buying some postcards, and they were not at all expensive. Deferring to Steve's impatience, she hurriedly selected a packet of cards, only to be greeted by a chorus of protests from all the peddlers whose souvenirs had been rejected. Smiling apologetically, Lila made her way through the knot of peddlers to join Steve at the table he had selected.

Once there, she ordered a cheese enchilada and a Coke, but as she and Steve waited for their food to arrive, she began to realise that recurring thoughts of Rafael were doing nothing for her appetite. She found herself dreading her return to his house. Obviously he could not be away from home all the time, and Lila was nervous at the thought of further encounters with him. It was clear that he cared nothing for her, and she was uncertain of how well she could conceal the mixture of emotions he had aroused in her. Rafael had awakened something in her that no man ever had, she admitted to herself, absently rubbing at the beads of moisture which had formed on her cold glass.

'I hope you weren't daydreaming like this during your exclusive tour,' came Steve's voice.

Lila jumped guiltily. 'Oh, I'm sorry, Steve. No, I can assure you, you had my rapt attention. Everything I learned this morning will help me a lot. In fact, I can hardly wait to put it to use.' She detected an uncertain smile on Steve's face and suddenly realised that he could have interpreted her last comment as a wish to bring their date to an end. She promptly made an effort to be more friendly, and soon they were chatting animatedly on a number of topics, not going into much of anything in depth. As Steve was telling her about some of his experiences in architecture school, Lila happened to catch a glimpse of something familiar out of the corner of one eye, and turned to see Rafael standing across the street. He was looking directly at her, but abruptly turned away as their eyes met. His angular features were harsh in the sunlight and even from the café she could see his jaws tighten. She frowned slightly, and looked down at her empty glass. An uneasy feeling suddenly enveloped her. Why should she care that Rafael had seen her with Steve ... except, she supposed, that it would probably only confirm his opinion of her as a shameless flirt.

Sensing that Lila was distracted, Steve said, 'You've never given me your phone number, you know. Where are you staying?'

Lila lowered her lashes. How could she explain her situation to Steve? 'Well, I ... I'm sort of between locations right now,' she replied after an awkward pause.

'I see,' Steve responded dejectedly, obviously feeling he had been snubbed.

Suddenly irritated by all the new complications in her life, Lila stood up. 'I think it's time I went back and started to work, Steve. Do you mind?'

'No, not at all.' Steve rose from his chair too, and reached into his hip pocket to pay the bill.

'Shall I walk you back?' he suggested.

Horrified at the prospect of him finding out that she was staying with a single man, Lila blurted, 'No—no, thanks. It's not too far.' She reached down to pick up her straw bag and notebook. 'Thanks again for everything.'

Things had certainly become complicated, she

thought as she walked back to Palmera for lunch. She had offended Steve because she didn't want him to know where she was staying. But even worse, Rafael would no doubt have some caustic remarks to make about her carrying on with yet another man. She had the choice of riding out the probable storm, or she could try to find a hotel somewhere, even if it weren't very convenient to the ruins. Something inside made her reluctant to move out, assuming she could find a place. But even though part of her wanted to be near Rafael, she knew it was in her best interests to stay somewhere else.

Over lunch, she decided to think more that afternoon about whether or not to leave. Certainly if she decided to, she couldn't make any more secret departures. She would have to tell Rafael face to face. She felt a quiver of nervous anticipation at the prospect.

In the meantime, she wanted to return to the ruins to make some sketches. She hurriedly collected her charcoal and paper. Standing in front of the large oval mirror, she braided her hair into two pigtails for coolness and topped them with an old straw hat she found on the closet shelf in her room. Feeling reasonably protected against the afternoon sun, she began her walk back.

Seated on a limestone outcropping that conveniently faced the Temple of the Dwarf, she was soon completely oblivious to the intense heat as she filled page after page with sketches. This was her first attempt at painting the monuments of a culture so removed in time and space from her own. It was going to be a challenge to capture its spirit, so she wanted to get the composition just right before she actually started painting. Frowning into the sun, she fell into a mood of intense concentration.

Finally noticing how much the shadows of the temples had lengthened before her, Lila glanced at her watch. It was already past the time when Maria said they usually had dinner. A hollowness began to invade her stomach as she quickly packed up her equipment. That was all she needed, to be late for dinner on top of having Rafael see her with Steve that afternoon. She didn't know for sure what his reaction would be to the afternoon, but having seen his face gave her a strong clue.

Her rush back to the house ended in a near-collision with Rafael as she burst through the front door. He appraised her coolly. 'I guess we can eat now that everyone is here. Carlos has been sitting at the table for quite a while now.'

It was true that she was late, but he certainly wasn't being the gracious host about it either. Lila suppressed a sarcastic response, and said civilly, 'Is there any time for me to get cleaned up and change my clothes?'

'Not unless you want to be rude,' Rafael replied curtly, and turned on his heel to go into the dining room. He looked immaculate in light blue slacks and a faintly striped shirt. Lila looked down at her slacks and tee-shirt. She was rather dusty and rumpled, but it appeared that she had no choice. She took her place at the table slowly, smiling gratefully at Carlos' excited greetings.

'It's the custom here to remove your hat at dinner. Or should I say my hat?' Rafael remarked, giving her a critical glance.

Lila slowly drew in her breath. She had no wish to start an argument with Rafael in front of his nephew, but it did seem to her that he was being outrageously rude. She was, after all, a guest in his home, not a wayward child. 'I'm very sorry I borrowed your hat without permission,' she said sarcastically as she removed it from her head. 'I do hope I haven't hurt it.' She gave Rafael a false, sweet smile and was rewarded with a glowering scowl.

Turning her attention to Carlos, Lila spent the remainder of the meal listening to his animated descriptions of the approaching Fiesta of San Cristoval in Merida. Rafael was silent throughout. Lila, unable to relax, barely tasted her food. She couldn't understand why Rafael was treating her this way. What had brought out this dark side of his nature again? Whatever the reason, his mercurial mood changes were only strengthening her inclination to leave and go to a hotel, and she resolved to mention it to him. As coffee was served and Carlos excused himself, she said timidly, 'Could I speak to you for a few moments?'

An abbreviated nod was the only reply she received, so she plunged ahead. 'I'm very grateful to you for letting me come here the other night. I needed a place to stay then, but now I think it's better if I leave. I'd like to go this evening if . . .'

'I'm afraid that's quite out of the question,' Rafael interrupted. His voice was steady, and his dark eyes looked directly into hers. 'I intend for you to stay here as long as you are in Uxmal.'

'You have no right to tell me where I'm going to stay!' Her fluttering eyelashes revealed her outrage. 'In case you hadn't noticed, I'm old enough to make those decisions for myself . . . and I've decided I would like to stay somewhere else.'

'Like with your boy-friend, I suppose?' Rafael's eyebrows rose cynically as he returned his cup to its saucer.

Lila felt her breath taken away. His remark caught her completely by surprise, though it shouldn't have. She had expected some consequences of his having seen her with Steve. Now it became completely clear why he had been so rude to her since she had returned. 'Maybe, yes, but that's strictly my business.' She managed a cool smile, hoping it would hide her wounded feelings.

'It is not strictly your business,' he said, bringing his fist into contact with the dining room table. 'You are living under my roof now. And the reason you're here is because of your damn foolishness.' He paused to let a sardonic grin creep over his angry face. 'Now, unless you feel you can't trust yourself with me here . . .'

Lila felt her face grow hot. The nerve of him! 'I think I can control myself,' she said slowly and distinctly, with undisguised sarcasm.

A smile slid across his face. 'I'm glad you've decided to stay. I'm leaving on an unexpected business trip next week, and I'll be out of town for almost two weeks. I don't like to leave Carlos alone with only the servants for company.' With these words, he pushed his chair from the table and strode from the room.

She stayed in the dining room, sipping at her coffee while Maria cleared the table. It was clear that Rafael wanted her to stay, but she could not imagine why. Surely it was not just that he wanted some companionship for Carlos. He had as much as told her she was not fit company for him. Still, she shrugged, if he would be away she might as well stay. His house was convenient to the ruins, and she could keep Carlos from feeling lonely in the evenings. At least if Rafael were gone, the tension she felt each time she entered the house would disappear. Perhaps most of the excitement would be gone as well, she thought briefly, then pushed the idea from her mind.

She gazed unseeing out the dining room window, her fingers circling her empty cup. It seemed Rafael was constantly disapproving of her. Nothing she did was right in his eyes. She tried to tell herself that his attitude didn't matter. After all, why should she care what he thought of her? But she had to admit that she did. It would be wonderful, just once, to be praised by him for something she did. She refused to pursue that thought, knowing from her experiences with her father the futility of such a hope.

Since the dinner hour was early and there was still plenty of light, Lila selected a book from Rafael's study and took it out to one of the lounge chairs on the terrace. She had become quite engrossed in the Spanish conquest of Latin America when she heard an angry male voice shouting her name. It couldn't be anyone but Rafael, although she hardly felt they were due for another argument. She closed the book and braced herself for combat.

Rafael came striding across the lawn, carrying a sketch pad and what seemed to be several sticks of charcoal. He was white-lipped with anger and Lila stood up to face him, unwilling to allow him to tower over her. Thrusting the charcoal under her nose, Rafael hissed, 'I thought I had made it perfectly clear that you were not to give Carlos your art supplies. I was not aware that there was any question in your mind about that. I can only conclude that you have deliberately disregarded my wishes.'

Lila was completely baffled and frowned up at him. 'I haven't the slightest idea what you're talking about,' she said dazedly. 'Are those mine?'

'Well, they are most definitely not mine,' Rafael

answered with a short bitter laugh. 'I don't think it strains the imagination too much to guess where they came from.'

'Weren't they in my painting bag?' Lila asked, still trying to understand what had happened.

'No, they were not,' Rafael exploded. 'I'm not in the habit of rummaging through your belongings. It's clear to me that you must have given them to Carlos. He was using them to make this.' With an angry snap of his wrist, Rafael flipped the sketch pad open to reveal a rough sketch of the front view of Palmera House.

Unable to resist, she said, 'It's a very good drawing, isn't it? He is quite talented, as I've said all along.'

A cynical grin appeared on his face. 'Here you are a guest in my house, you violate my expressed wishes, and you don't feel the slightest bit apologetic about it.'

'No, Rafael,' Lila replied softly, 'because I never gave them to Carlos.'

Rafael's eyes bored into her own. 'I don't know whether to believe you or not.'

Lila drew herself erect. It hadn't ever occurred to her that Rafael might not believe her. 'Just because you believe I have loose morals it doesn't mean I'm a liar too, you know. It may surprise you, but even artists have some standards.' She had managed to respond evenly, though inside she was anything but calm. Anyone else's unfavourable opinions she would have been able to shrug off, but Rafael always managed to wound her.

'Oh, they have standards all right. It's just that they're different from the ones most of us have. Let's see, they never like to have more than two or three lovers at one time, and . . .'

His speech was cut short by Carlos, who just then approached him. Guessing that Carlos wanted to talk to Rafael privately, Lila picked up her book and moved to a spot out of hearing range. She sat on the grass and opened her book, but found her attention straying to their conversation. They were talking too quietly for her to hear, but she guessed that Carlos was explaining to Rafael that she had not given him the equipment.

Carlos was shamefaced and stared fixedly at the gravel beneath his feet. Lila felt sorry for him. He was very talented and wanted so much to draw. She wondered if she herself would be an artist now if she had met the kind of discouragement Carlos was meeting. She looked up as Rafael sat down next to her.

'I would like to offer my apologies,' he said hesitantly. His dark eyes were cast down in embarrassment. Being wrong was undoubtedly an unfamiliar experience for him, and Lila couldn't help responding to his distress. 'It's all right, really, I . . .'

'No, it isn't all right.' He stretched his hand over hers. 'I should have believed you. Anyway, not only did I falsely accuse you, I find that my

nephew actually took the things from your bag
without permission. He knows better.'

'Don't you think he took them just because he
wants so badly to paint?' Lila asked, thinking that
this might be a good moment to intercede for
Carlos.

'What an eight-year-old wants is, I'm afraid,
not always in his best interests. I think I'm in a
better position to make that judgment, and I feel
too strongly about this issue to change my views.
I hope you understand, Lila.'

She felt an involuntary quiver of excitement.
This was the first time he had called her by name.
She knew it meant nothing to him. Tomorrow he
could just as easily return her to anonymous
status. Still . . .

CHAPTER SEVEN

AFTER an early breakfast by herself the next morning, Lila returned to the ruins. The morning was marred only by the appearance of Steve leading a tour group. He greeted her a little tentatively, and Lila found herself responding effusively to make up for having hurt his feelings the previous day. Despite her efforts, Steve had seemed reserved and sulky. Afterwards, Lila decided it was just as well. She really wasn't interested in Steve, so there was no reason to try to develop the scant relationship they had established. Still, she felt awkward and guilty after the encounter, and it took her some time to once again become engrossed in her work.

As the heat of the day became intense, she stopped work and returned to the house. She had decided the best plan was to work through lunch each day rather than walk back and forth twice. That way she would at least not run the risk of being late for dinner. After taking a shower and changing into clean tangerine slacks and a suntop, Lila decided to wander in the gardens. She stopped to tell Maria where she was going, then crossed the terrace and walked through a small break in an oleander hedge.

She was amused to observe that Rafael's garden was as different from Françoise's as the two owners were. Where Françoise's garden was a chaotic blend of every conceivable colour and scent, Rafael's was carefully laid out, with each area separated by a neatly-trimmed hedge. It was really a formal English-style garden, and she concluded that Rafael's grandfather must have planned it. It was as out of keeping with Uxmal as Palmera was.

Lila heard a distant, boyish voice crying, 'Guess what! Guess what!' and the sound of running feet announced Carlos' arrival in the garden. Lila smiled to herself as Carlos rushed madly to and fro, unable to see her because of the tall hedges that divided the garden. Finally he appeared breathlessly in front of her. 'We're going to the fiesta this evening! Uncle Rafael says we can have an early dinner and then go.'

'Oh, that's wonderful, Carlos. I hope you have a wonderful time,' Lila replied.

'But you're coming too. My uncle said so.' Carlos paused as a slight frown appeared on his forehead. 'Unless you don't want to go. Oh, please come! This is the last day of the fiesta—the best of all. They have a parade, and fireworks and everything. Oh yeah, and the grown-ups have a dance.'

She considered a moment. The prospect of an evening with Rafael made her feel a little shaky. Carlos' enthusiasm, while enormous, could not be expected to tide her and Rafael over the conflicts that inevitably seemed to arise between them. Besides, she certainly wouldn't want him to have the idea that she was seeking his company by going. Lila could tell by Carlos' wide hopeful eyes, however, that he would be very disappointed if she didn't go, and that turned the balance.

'I'd love to come,' said Lila, patting his shoulder fondly.

'Oh, boy! See you in a few minutes—don't take long, okay?'

On the way upstairs, Lila began to consider what she would wear, and it struck her that the skirt and blouse she had bought in Merida would be perfect for the occasion. She had thought her purchase an indulgence at the time, although it had been a good bargain. Now, it was going to come in handy, since none of the clothes she had brought would have been quite right.

As she pulled the peasant skirt and blouse from the closet, however, she couldn't help comparing them against Stephanie's clothes hanging alongside. Until that moment, she'd been excited about her new outfit. Now she suddenly felt that no matter what she wore, she would be almost drab compared to Stephanie. There was no question about it, Rafael Blake went for the exotic type, and that certainly wasn't Lila. He must think her very dull by comparison.

She moved away from the closet, shrugging impatiently. Why should she be comparing herself to Rafael's girl-friend, anyway? His love life certainly was of no importance to her.

After dressing, she applied a light covering of make-up. The light green eye shadow heightened the intensity of her turquoise eyes, and her lips glowed alluringly under her frosted rose lip cream. She stood back to inspect her appearance in the mirror, and was pleased with herself after all.

'Good evening,' Rafael murmured when he saw her. His gaze lingered at the lace border of her neckline, which extended slightly below her tan and revealed glimpses of creamy-white skin. 'I can see I'm going to be the envy of all the men this evening. But I hope, since I'm taking you, you'll manage to save a dance or two for me.'

He gave a wide smile, which sent Lila's heart racing. There was something about the sensuous curve of his mouth that took her breath away. She couldn't remember his ever having smiled at her before. She recovered her composure in time to banter with him. 'Maybe you'd better take along a sword to fend off the hordes of suitors!'

By the time they arrived in Merida, the intense heat of the day had passed and a suggestion of the moon was visible over the low palm trees. The streets cordoned off for the procession were adorned with branches, and the balconies of several of the houses were hung with silk banners proclaiming the festival. The most striking attraction, peculiar to the Yucatan, was the horse-drawn

carriages that had been saved from decades ago
and were now used only for the Festival. The carriages were painted a bright crimson and each was
occupied by two or three ladies dressed in colourful native costumes.

Lila wandered towards the large wooden platform that had been set up for outdoor dancing,
while Rafael excused himself to get Carlos settled
in with some friends to watch the fireworks. The
orchestra was playing waltz music and Lila
watched the feet of the dancers as they fell to the
rhythm of the music's gentle cadence. As she
watched the platform, her gaze was drawn involuntarily to Rafael's returning figure. Somehow
he stood out in the crowd, and it wasn't simply
because of his slick light brown leather sport coat
and indigo shirt open at the neck. She couldn't
help noticing that hers wasn't the only female
head to be drawn by his purely masculine appeal.

He had a drink in each hand, and offered one
to Lila. 'You know, as much as Carlos has been
looking forward to the fiesta, I doubt he would
have come if you hadn't agreed to come along.'
His mouth twisted slightly at the corners, and he
took a long draught from his glass. 'You seem to
have a nice touch with children.'

Lila was a little taken aback. This was the
second compliment he had given her tonight, and
she wasn't sure how to respond. 'You sound surprised,' she said finally, her chin noticeably
raised.

'To the extent that I'm capable of that emotion, I guess I am. It seems to be passé these days to be interested in family life—especially among liberated women such as yourself,' he added with a mocking grin.

So that was how he thought of her. His attitudes about women sounded about as up to date as Palmera House, she thought, and sought to control her rising temperature by taking a sip of her Margarita. 'It sounds as if you prefer the *un*liberated type—the kind you can keep under your thumb, perhaps.'

'Not at all,' he asserted calmly. 'But I'm just old-fashioned enough to prefer feminine women.'

Inside, a small voice was screaming, 'Here I am, I'm feminine.' But she controlled the urge to prove herself worthy of his attentions and replied, 'Are you implying that liberated women aren't feminine?' She didn't really want to hear what she felt certain his answer would be.

He evaded answering her question, responding instead with one of his own. 'Do you consider yourself something of an expert on femininity?'

'Well, I am a woman, and . . .'

'It takes a man to recognise that quality in a woman,' Rafael interrupted, his ebony gaze piercing her fluttering lashes like the beam of a laser.

As they stood in awkward silence and finished their drinks, Lila could feel her spirits begin to plunge. Obviously he didn't think of her as feminine. Apparently he thought it wasn't possible to have a career and be feminine as well. Unbidden, the image of Stephanie pushed its way into her mind, and brought a stab of anguish.

Of course! Stephanie didn't have to lower herself by working for a living, and obviously spared no expense or energy in making herself look appealing. The image was strangely disquieting, and she found herself wishing that Rafael were not standing within inches of her at this moment.

As if he had read her mind, Rafael stepped away to talk with a large, ruddy-faced man, leaving Lila on her own.

It's just as well, she thought, twisting her mouth sarcastically. If he thinks I'm unfeminine, then he certainly shouldn't be obliged to spend any more time with me than is politely necessary. She fixed her gaze on the dancers, feigning an interest that would disguise her wounded pride. Sensing a light touch of feminine fingers on her arm, she turned, to find herself facing Françoise.

'Françoise, what a surprise,' she blurted. What would Françoise think of her now?

'I saw you quite a while ago,' Françoise whispered conspiratorially, 'but I had to pick my moment to talk to you. And now you are alone.' She smiled knowingly. 'Still waters run deep, eh? Who would have thought you were such a fast worker? I told you he is a fine catch. Just make sure you have him truly hooked,' she added, winking subtly.

Lila shook her head dumbly and tried to respond. 'Françoise, it isn't like that at all. In fact . . .'

'I saw the way he looks at you when you are unaware. I think you have nothing to worry about.'

Lila found it hard to believe that Françoise wasn't angry about her mysterious midnight exit from her house. 'Françoise,' she began hesitantly, 'you must think I'm a very ungrateful guest. I'm really very sorry about sneaking out the way I did.' She turned her glass awkwardly in her hand, unable to meet the other woman's gaze.

Françoise made a comical face. 'I was surprised, yes. But when I was your age, I too did some unexpected things. And now that I have seen you with Rafael Blake, I understand why you left. Who can resist the call of the heart?'

So Françoise thought she had left because she wanted to move in with Rafael! Well, it was better than having her guess the truth about Georges, Lila decided. She was grateful that Françoise was being so understanding, even if she had a false idea of the circumstances under which Lila had left.

'Well, I hope my running off didn't upset your plans,' Lila said apologetically. 'I can see now that it was foolish of me to be in such a hurry.'

Françoise patted her arm reassuringly. 'Don't give it another thought. You have not created any problems for me. But now I must rush back to Armando, my new friend—he'll be wondering

what has happened to me. You must come over
for a swim some afternoon!'

Bemused by Françoise's easy acceptance of
her behaviour, Lila stared blindly at her retreating form until she could no longer locate her in
the crowd. She turned back to Rafael and saw
that he was still engaged in conversation, his back
to her.

Several minutes passed, all the while Lila's
anger at being left making its inexorable assent.
She reminded herself that he hadn't been away all
that long, and that part of the time she had been
talking to Françoise anyway. But her efforts at
control were futile. She knew that it wasn't being
left alone that bothered her, but the fact that
Rafael was ignoring her and seemed quite happy
to be spending the time with others as if she
weren't there. Finally, her internal fury demand-
ing some action, she turned on her heel to seek
other company. She would show him!

Almost in answer to her quest, Steve's blond
hair appeared amidst a knot of people in her path.
With a reckless gleam in her eyes, she accepted
Steve's invitation to dance, and found herself
moving slowly around the wooden platform.
Steve's touch was tentative and Lila found it difficult to follow his lead. Frowning a little with
concentration, she glanced at the crowd over
Steve's shoulder. Rafael drew her eyes as
naturally as if she had been in a spotlight. He was
alone now and staring straight at her. The firm

set of his shoulders was enough to reveal his displeasure.

The full measure of her retaliation not yet spent, Lila remained with Steve at the side of the platform opposite Rafael, then they danced together again. Afterwards, Steve led her to a group of his friends, who were local travel agents and tour guides. She stayed until Steve was involved in conversation with the group, then excused herself, aware that the longer she stayed away, the more she was courting disaster.

When she returned to Rafael's side, she was greeted with an angry frown. 'Everywhere I have travelled, it is the custom to stay with the person who brings you to a dance. Apparently this is not true in your circles.'

'You didn't stay with me,' she retorted. 'Why should I stand around waiting for you to finish talking with your friends?'

Rafael's eyebrows lifted in a way she was beginning to recognise, and to dread. 'If you would prefer to go home with your boy-friend,' he spat out, making the single word carry the weight of a violent charge against her morals, 'you are free to do so.'

Lila felt her throat tighten in anger. 'I wouldn't want to disappoint Carlos,' she replied in even, scalding tones.

Rafael ignored her sarcasm. 'By the way, have you thought to tell your friend where you are staying?'

'I haven't mentioned it,' Lila acknowledged quietly, not wanting to continue this particular subject.

'Aha!' Rafael exclaimed in amusement. 'So even artists have some concept of propriety. I must admit I'm surprised to hear it.'

'Given the way you feel about artists, I am at a loss to understand why you insist upon my staying at your house,' said Lila, growing furious at his unending attacks on her. 'Surely you could find someone with more suitable values to stay with Carlos while you're gone.'

'To be perfectly frank, I'm beginning to question that decision myself,' Rafael shot back.

'Well, I'm getting sick and tired of your insults and insinuations and I . . .' She stopped mid-sentence as the smiling face of a strange man appeared directly in front of her.

'I don't believe we've been introduced,' the stranger said, glancing meaningfully at Rafael.

'Franklin Myers, Lila Fleming,' Rafael replied tonelessly, his face devoid of expression.

Lila glanced curiously at her new acquaintance, taking in his thinning brown hair and small moustache. Rafael's expressionless face suggested that he disliked or disapproved of him. Perhaps he was an artist, she smiled to herself.

'Now that we've been properly introduced,' said Franklin, 'may I have this dance?' He placed his hand on Lila's arm as if to lead her away. Rafael frowned at her sternly and gave his head a slight shake. She hadn't really wanted to dance with this man, but her feeling that Rafael was trying to tell her what to do rekindled the flames of her anger.

Lila smiled mischievously up at Franklin. 'I'd love to dance,' she murmured, and allowed him to steer her to the far side of the platform. As the music began, Franklin pulled her uncomfortably close. Lila pressed her hand firmly against his shoulder in an attempt to keep him at a distance, but Franklin resisted her efforts. He moved his head close to hers and she turned away quickly to avoid being cheek to cheek.

She looked pleadingly over Franklin's left shoulder at Rafael, and with an angry gesture he put down his drink and moved across the dance floor to tap Franklin on the shoulder. 'I'll cut in now,' he said evenly. 'I haven't had an opportunity to dance with Lila yet this evening.'

Franklin gave a resigned shrug as Rafael grasped Lila firmly about the waist and spun her away. 'I suppose you enjoyed that,' he said, with a sardonic grin.

'Of course not,' she replied, widening her eyes and gazing up at him as if her astonishment were too great to contain. 'How could you imagine I would enjoy dancing with someone like that?'

'Actually,' Rafael responded evenly, 'I wasn't referring to the dance. I meant that you apparently enjoyed rejecting my advice.'

'I didn't take it as advice,' said Lila, a little

sheepishly, realising that she had overreacted to his gesture.

'The man is notorious. No one who knows him wants to dance with him, so he has to search out naïve newcomers like yourself to pester. I did my best to spare you the experience, but like most people of "artistic" temperament, you seem set on your own private vision of the world, and can't profit from anyone else's wisdom.'

Lila's back stiffened under his hand as she glared at Rafael. 'You spend a lot of time making insulting generalisations about artists based on your brother-in-law! According to you, we're a socially irresponsible lot, without morals and I don't know what else. Well, at least my paintings give other people enjoyment.' Aware that the words on the tip of her tongue would only further goad his anger, she was unable to halt their reckless escape. 'I'm not sure what *you* contribute. You own the land others farm. Do you consider that a contribution?'

A vein in Rafael's forehead began to pulse, and she could feel the muscles of his arm tense against her back. Fearing that she had gone too far, Lila felt a stab of anxiety. In staccato speech that revealed his obvious effort at control, Rafael said, 'As if it were any business of yours, I think I treat my tenants quite fairly. They get a good price for their sisal—in bad years, I have paid them more than the market price. They come to me for help with their family problems. And I'm certainly not dependent upon their labour for my livelihood.'

Lila continued, somehow daring to push him further, as if all her pent-up anger and resentment were finding an unexpected vent. 'Françoise told me you did nothing to help the new medical clinic. You call her frivolous and even worse, but at least she contributed something to the clinic besides going to the party!'

Rafael looked at her evenly. 'Lila, you have no idea what you're talking about.' His hand tightened on her fingers as his other arm pulled her closer as if to close the conversation.

Lila found she needed all her attention to follow Rafael's increasingly difficult moves. He pressed her tightly against his chest and whirled her around the dance floor. It was almost as if he were challenging her or testing her, she thought, but she relaxed against him, allowing his hand on her back to guide her.

Their bodies were pressed together now, and Lila's pulse was beating more quickly. Enjoying the faint sensation of his warm breath fluttering her hair, she had a feeling of floating, as if they were alone in space instead of dancing on a crowded platform. She imagined that they could stay like this for ever. When the music stopped, Lila was unwilling to break the spell and failed to pull away from him. She tilted her head and gazed up at him, finding a quizzical smile on his face.

'It's too bad you find it necessary to argue all

the time. You're much more alluring when you're not talking.' Rafael grinned as Lila pushed him away angrily. All her fantasies came crashing down around her. 'I think it's time we left. Carlos must be exhausted.'

Lila could think of nothing less appealing than a ride home with Rafael after his last remark. But it was too far to walk, especially in the dark. She sighed. At least Carlos would be there to prevent them from having any further arguments. She trailed after Rafael while he located Carlos and returned to the car. Carlos, initially full of chatter about the fireworks and the parade, soon succumbed to the tense atmosphere and fell silent. Once inside the house, the three parted quickly and disappeared into their rooms.

Lila paced her room wearily. Why did she and Rafael always seem to be arguing? It was hard to remember their few friendly conversations. Rafael always assumed the worst about her, it seemed, and he also had a disturbing way of bringing out her least attractive qualities. Never in her life had she spoken to anyone the way she had spoken to Rafael tonight. It was strange that despite all their conflicts, Rafael wanted her to stay on at his house. But even more curious was that somehow she was beginning to feel as if she belonged here. Almost two weeks had gone by, and she had not intended to stay much longer than a month. The thought of leaving was now inexplicably disturbing.

CHAPTER EIGHT

THE next few days were sultry. Lila's long heavy hair became a burden to her, even when pinned on top of her head. Her cheeks glowed from the heat and her usually brisk step became heavy and sedate. The daily walk to and from the ruins remained pleasant in the morning, but the return walk in the afternoon was an ordeal. Arriving flushed at the house on Friday, Lila was startled to find Françoise in conversation with Maria in the entry hall.

'There you are, my dear!' she exclaimed, throwing her arms wide. 'I've come to make good my invitation to come over for an afternoon swim. The pool is the only place to be on a day like this.'

'Do you think I could come, too, Lila?' Carlos had been taking in the conversation from the dining room. He turned to Françoise with a pleading expression. 'Can I?'

'Of course you are invited.' Françoise gave Carlos a wide smile. 'What is your name, my friend?' As Carlos and Françoise got acquainted, Lila had a few moments of indecision. Given Rafael's attitude towards Françoise, she was pretty sure he would not want Carlos to be at her house, although obviously no harm would come to him there. Also, after her experience with Georges, she had no desire to meet Armando, whoever he might be.

'You will come, won't you?' Françoise turned back to Lila. 'It's no fun to swim alone.'

'Isn't Armando there?' Lila asked as airily as she could.

'Armando left yesterday and I have been rattling around the house with nothing to do. So! What is your answer?'

The prospect of a swim was suddenly much more inviting. 'Yes, we'd love to come,' Lila decided. 'Just give me time to shower and put on my suit.'

'I'll go back to my house and tell Rosa to make some lemonade and get out some homemade cookies,' Françoise answered cheerfully. 'Just come straight back to the pool when you arrive.'

Carlos dashed headlong to his room to change. When Lila returned to the front of the house a few minutes later clad in her patterned green suit and matching wraparound skirt, Carlos was already waiting impatiently. He bounced up and down restlessly while she checked to be sure he had remembered his towel and thongs, and then scampered ahead of her through the dense woods.

As they passed the bench where Georges had found her the night of Françoise's party, Lila shivered lightly as if she had been touched by a cold draught. She pictured Rafael towering angrily over her; his fingers biting into her shoulders. And then, unexpectedly, came the memory of his kiss that night, and its effect on her.

'Lila!' said Carlos. 'Aren't you listening?'

She shook her head to bring herself back to the present and saw Carlos frowning at her in exasperation. 'I'm sorry, Carlos. Were you talking to me?'

'Yes, I wondered if Señora Miguel's pool has a diving board.'

'I don't think so,' Lila replied.

'It doesn't really matter,' Carlos said cheerfully. 'I just wanted to practise some dives.'

As they came to a clear view of the pool, Carlos broke into a run. Lila remembered with a sudden stab of apprehension that she hadn't even asked Carlos if he could swim, and hurried after him. Her fears were quickly relieved—Carlos could swim like a porpoise. While Françoise and Lila were content to paddle tamely around on inflated rafts, chatting and keeping cool, Carlos was constantly in vigorous motion. By the end of the afternoon, as ragged banners of ivory clouds began to obscure the sun, everyone was pleasantly tired. At Lila's insistence, she and Carlos returned in plenty of time to clean up and dress for dinner. She definitely did not want another quarrel with Rafael.

Lila was chatting with Carlos and helping Maria put the last few dishes on the table when Rafael walked into the dining room. His familiar scent—a masculine mixture of shaving lotion and soap—was sufficient to alert all her senses. She would have been keenly aware of his presence, even if she hadn't heard the chair scrape across the oak floor as he drew it back to sit down.

Unconsciously aware that she didn't want Carlos to talk about the afternoon, Lila was uncharacteristically talkative. She carried on about the food through the green chili soup and stuffed quail, then went on to chat about the sultry weather, and whatever else popped into her head. But it was all to no avail. When the first conversational gap occurred, Carlos chimed into tell Rafael about their visit to Françoise's pool.

At Carlos's mention of the afternoon's events, Rafael stiffened visibly. Not surprisingly, Rafael disapproved of his going to Françoise's house and he would hold her responsible. Her glance slid towards Rafael across the table. 'Could we talk later?' she asked, a pleading note in her voice. At least, she hoped, she would spare Carlos the argument. There was no reason to ruin his day after he had enjoyed himself so much. He need never know how much trouble his desire to go had caused.

Rafael hesitated perceptibly, then replied, 'Of course,' and nodded.

Lila's usually hearty appetite suddenly disappeared in expectation of the lecture she was to receive after dinner. As much as it went against her grain, she resolved to apologise. After all,

Rafael was in charge of Carlos and she was not. She really had no right to violate Rafael's wishes where Carlos was concerned, and in her heart she had known he would not want him to visit Françoise's house.

'Maria tells me you spend time at the ruins every day,' Rafael said as if making polite conversation with a stranger.

'Yes,' Lila replied hesitantly. It was a little difficult to talk freely when she was all but forbidden to discuss her painting in front of Carlos.

'I've been quite interested in the ruins myself,' he said amiably. 'It was a fascinating culture that produced these temples, although deciphering its mysteries has been challenging, since almost all the Mayan books were burned by a fanatic Spanish bishop in the sixteenth century.'

'Yes,' said Lila, keeping alive the opportunity to hear more. 'It seems people know very little about the cultural aspects of the temples.' She began picturing the structures she had been painting. 'Like the Temple of the Dwarf . . . how did it get its name, do you know?'

'Yes, it's from a Mayan legend. An old Mayan witch succeeded in hatching a child from a serpent's egg, and within a year the infant grew to manhood but in the body of a dwarf. When the year ended, the witch sent the dwarf out to defy the gods and with her help he erected this incredible temple in a single night . . . that's why there is the small statue of a dwarf on the temple wall.'

Carlos had finished his dinner and was focusing wide-eyed on Rafael as he continued to relate his seemingly boundless knowledge of the Mayan culture.

'One of the amazing things is that they created a flourishing, highly developed culture with very few resources. There was no salt nearby, no metal, and no rivers for easy travel. In fact, lack of water was a severe problem for the Maya.'

'What did they do?' Carlos asked. 'You have to have water.'

Rafael smiled indulgently. 'They had both a spiritual and practical approach to that problem,' he said. 'They believed in the powers of their gods to bring rain, and they formed their cities around *cenotes* ... like the one you visit down the road.' He looked at Carlos.

Lila and Carlos eyed one another, both remembering that that was where they had met each other.

'The ancients used to throw virgins into the sacred *cenotes* to appease their gods and bring more rain.'

'I guess Lila better not be hanging around the *cenotes* by herself,' Carlos said between giggles. 'She might get thrown in.'

Rafael grinned as he set down his coffee cup. 'I don't think there's any danger of that,' he quipped, apparently confident that Carlos wouldn't understand his meaning.

Lila gulped her coffee so quickly it scalded her

throat. She could hardly respond to his crack in front of Carlos. She glanced at the boy and saw that he had nearly finished his dessert. Soon, she knew, he would excuse himself and she would be alone with Rafael. The dinner had passed quite pleasantly except for the hidden insult, and she had to admit she had learned more about the Mayan culture by listening to Rafael than she had since she had been in the Yucatan. She dared to hope Rafael would forget their agreement to talk after dinner.

As Carlos excused himself, she lifted her cup with trembling fingers, taking pains to avoid Rafael's eyes. How she dreaded another argument! Perhaps it would be best to start right off by admitting that she had been wrong. Rafael's voice came suddenly, startling her so that she choked on her coffee.

'Lila, I don't want to argue with you, especially since this is my last night at home for a while.' His dark eyes sought hers before continuing. 'But while I am away, I would prefer that Carlos did not visit at Françoise Miguel's house again. I'm sure she has some good qualities, but the parade of male visitors to her house over the last several years has been quite astonishing. I really don't think she is a suitable companion for Carlos—or for you for that matter.'

Lila was wide-eyed. She had been prepared for his anger; she was used to that. But the quiet, almost trusting tone was new and caught her off guard. And the way he had looked at her had melted any desire for protective armour. 'I will see to that,' she said, 'I'm sorry I let him go today.' Although she hated to admit it, she felt that Rafael was right. Françoise had certainly been kind to her, but she did seem indifferent to conventional morality and made no effort to protect her reputation.

Rafael barely suppressed a smile. 'I know how difficult it can be to refuse Carlos something he wants.'

Ridiculously, Lila felt tears prickling her eyelids. 'Have a good trip,' she blurted, as she blinked to hold back her tears. She pushed back her chair and hurriedly left the room before she was betrayed by her emotions. What in the world was she crying about anyway? It couldn't be that she was sorry Rafael was going away, she reasoned. After all, hadn't she done her best to avoid him much of the time? Now at least she would be able to do as she pleased without his interference and constant disapproval. And when he returned, it would be nearly time for her to leave. So why the tears? The only explanation that presented itself was that she had been momentarily thrown off balance by his softness.

In her room, Lila tried to control her tangled mass of emotions by looking through her work on the ruins. Usually, focusing on her work helped to calm her down. Besides, she hadn't yet sat down and looked through all her work at one time.

Spreading her canvases out on the patterned
Indian rug for a critical appraisal, she detected a
certain monotony. All showed a scorching sun,
creating an impression of intense heat. She had
varied the composition, but not the colours.
Vegetation, sun, and stone, the same greens and
greys echoed in all she had done. For the second
time that evening, Lila felt close to tears. The
work she had started just would not be sufficient.
She should have seen earlier that she needed more
variety. True, she had the two paintings she had
done before she went to the ruins. At least they
added a new dimension. And the portrait of
Rafael. But that was private. That painting would
never be in a show.

Lila sat cross-legged on the window seat, gazing
out at the evening sky, and mulling over the
problem of how to get more variety into her
paintings of the ruins. The sunset was a strange,
pinkish orange, broken up by large dark areas of
clouds. That was it! The solution to her problem
was suddenly obvious. She stuffed her supplies
into her canvas bag and dashed down the stairs.
In the yard she encountered Carlos, who was
pursuing some sort of moth.

'Lila!' he called in surprise. 'Where are you
going?'

'The ruins,' she answered without slowing. She
would have to hurry to catch the light. The roses
and charcoals in the sky, the new shadows, would
create a picture with a darker, more mysterious

atmosphere. The hues would express perfectly the enigma of the lost, ancient culture.

Breathless by the time she arrived at the ruins, she tried to mix her colours as carefully as if she had all the time in the world. The angry sky, which formed a backdrop to the Temple of the Dwarf, was as promising as she had hoped, and she probably would never have a better chance to capture it.

She was brushing in the clouds with hurried strokes when she felt a drop of rain on the back of her hand. She looked up at the sky. The blue was shrinking, giving way to the steadily advancing layer of storm clouds. There was little time left. Swiftly she sketched in the massive structure, then turned to find exactly the right colour for the long eerie shadows that stretched from it. She continued working intently, ignoring the increasing frequency of the raindrops, until the light was too poor to continue. Lila began to pack up her equipment, hoping she had managed to start something that would still seem worthwhile in the light of day. By now the back of her thin cotton blouse, which had been exposed to the rain, had become saturated, and clung to her skin. In her haste, she had not stopped to think about bringing a jacket.

As she turned to make sure she had left nothing behind, her sandal slipped on a wet rock and her ankle twisted so painfully that an anguished cry broke from her lips. She poked tentatively at her throbbing ankle. The pain subsided only when she held her foot very still. When she tried to stand up, the searing pains shot up her leg.

She was beginning to get anxious about being out in a storm at night. Unfamiliar with the local climate, she had no way of knowing how intense the storm would be or how long it would last. She was ready to try almost any means she could think of for getting back to Palmera. She could try hopping home on one foot. Clutching her paint bag firmly in one hand, she cautiously attempted one hop, only to slip again on the wet stone. As she instinctively used her injured foot to save herself from falling, the ankle gave way and she collapsed again.

Biting her lip with pain and vexation, she sat back against the rock. There didn't seem to be any way of getting back home as long as the ground was slippery. She would have to stay where she was, probably until morning, since no one would miss her. Carlos would have gone to bed and, for all Rafael knew, she was in her room. As soon as the first tourists started arriving, she would be able to find someone to help her home.

Despite her efforts to remain calm and sensible, Lila was overcome by a wave of loneliness and self-pity. It was an eerie place to spend the night alone. Already she could imagine how slowly each minute would pass. She couldn't imagine falling asleep; her wet clothes and throbbing ankle would keep her awake even if the hard stone did not. She gingerly picked up her foot and tried to prop it on top of her canvas bag.

She noticed that the rain seemed to be subsiding. Unfortunately, she was already so drenched that it didn't make much difference. All was silent, save the elusive cry of a solitary night bird. She sat in almost total darkness, the outlines of the surrounding temples barely visible. She noticed a round faint light bobbing up and down in the distance, and for a moment, hope surged that someone would find her. Then the light seemed to swerve away from her and disappear into the blackness. Probably a bicycle along the road, she thought dejectedly.

'Lila! Lila!' a deep male voice called.

'Here!' she called back, trying to keep her voice from becoming too shrill. Within seconds she saw Rafael walking quickly towards her holding a flashlight which suddenly shone on her. In the light, she noticed with embarrassment that the rain had made her blouse transparent, and she folded her arms in an inadequate gesture to cover her breasts.

His eyes strayed down to her wet blouse before he said, 'Carlos got worried when the rains began and wanted me to bring the car here to meet you. He didn't want you to get too wet.' He smiled wryly, seeming to find her condition mildly entertaining. 'I expected to meet you on the road. Why are you still here?'

Feeling a little foolish, she looked up at him and said, 'I slipped and twisted my ankle.' She pointed to her bare foot. 'I think it must be sprained. I couldn't walk on it.'

She barely had time to grab her painting bag before she was lifted in Rafael's arms. She was immediately aware of the warmth of his body through her wet clothes. It seemed as though their bare skin was touching, and her heart began to race. Part of her wanted him to keep pressing against her for ever.

Seeming unaware of her emotions, Rafael carried her to his car and carefully settled her in the front seat. As he started the engine, he remarked, 'I know you're cold, but I'm not going to turn on the heat. It's such a short ride, it would only create a cold draught and make you feel worse. Besides,' he added, reaching over to touch her nose lightly with his fingertip, 'it might dry your blouse.' With reddened face, Lila looked down and abruptly returned her arms across her chest.

When they arrived at the house and Rafael picked her up again, she pressed against him, feeling that her chattering teeth gave her some licence. He was very strong, she thought as he carried her up the . stairs. She could feel the muscles of his body moving against her skin.

As he walked past the door to her room, Lila's heart began to thump heavily. Where was he taking her? 'Rafael?' she said softly, not wanting to appear naïve.

'I have a small sitting room at the end of the hall. There's a fire in the fireplace there to warm you up.' He smiled down at her almost tenderly, she thought, as he opened the door.

Lila found herself lying on an over-stuffed corduroy sofa in front of the fire while Rafael disappeared into the next room. Returning with a soft flannel robe, he said, 'Give me your wet things and I'll put them in the laundry room for Maria. You can wear this robe, it's quite warm.'

Lila accepted the robe, then looked up at Rafael hesitantly. He smiled in a way that told her he had read her thoughts, and reluctantly turned to leave.

After the door had closed, she removed her wet clothes and underthings. Her nakedness in one of Rafael's rooms gave her an overpowering feeling of exposure and vulnerability. She had barely gathered the robe about her and joined the ties at the waist when a knock at the door announced his return.

He entered without waiting for a reply, and held up an elastic bandage. 'This should make it possible for you to hobble around without too much pain.' He gestured to her to sit on the couch and knelt on the floor in front of her, deftly winding the bandage around her slim ankle. The feel of his gentle touch on her bare leg was enough to make her catch her breath with excitement. She wondered if he could hear her heart thundering inside her.

Rafael stood and offered his hands, and she willingly relied on his strength to pull herself off the sofa without putting weight on her foot. Gingerly she stood on both feet, and found she could even take a quick step forward without too much discomfort. She smiled up at Rafael gratefully, and before she had a chance to realise what was happening, she was suddenly enveloped in his arms. His lips brushed hers, their light and inviting touch sending her blood racing. As he drew back, her lashes fluttered open to gaze into the warmth of his dark eyes. She moaned as he pulled her close against him. The softness of his touch inflamed her in a way she had not thought possible. She felt as though the room were swirling around her. Her lips parted involuntarily, bringing a rapturous intimacy she had never known. She felt his breathing quicken and knew that he was as aroused as she. He pressed himself against her until she felt that an electric current held them together.

Unresisting, she allowed Rafael to lower her slowly to the sofa. He drew back to look at her, the firelight playing on his smooth forehead. Slowly he removed her bracelet, then her earrings, and dropped them to the floor. She was completely naked now underneath his thin robe. Unable to resist his overpowering sensuality, she put her hands on his shoulders to pull him close against her. She was vaguely aware that the neck of the robe had fallen open, and her skin was

burning beneath his gaze. Rafael murmured her
name in a husky voice as he nibbled kisses behind
her ear and down her throat, and Lila stroked his
hair in an ecstasy of sensuality. Her body was on
fire with his kisses.

She gave a trembling sigh as he drew the lapels
of the robe farther apart. His hands caressed the
soft, yielding shape of her, inviting her total surrender. His lips and his hands were sending her
to the height of ecstasy. As his fingers found the
knot in the sash of the robe, she whispered his
name pleadingly. 'Rafael, I've never . . .'

'I know, sweetheart, don't worry.' Rafael's lips
sought hers again as if to reassure her. The
pounding of Lila's heart was so loud, she at first
did not hear the sound that made him tense and
draw away from her.

With an exasperated sigh, he stood up and ran
his fingers through his tousled hair. Lila realised
that someone had been knocking on the door to
the room for several seconds. Suddenly aware of
her situation, she sat up quickly and pulled the
robe tightly about her. She wished desperately for
her clothes, wet as they were. As Rafael spoke
quietly to someone outside the door, Lila stood in
front of the fire, unable to control the shivering
that had suddenly overcome her. She felt naked
and defenceless, having completely let down her
guard for a man whom she knew would never
value her.

Hearing Rafael's return, she spun around

swiftly, her arms wrapped protectively across her chest. 'That was Carlos,' Rafael told her with a light smile. 'He couldn't sleep until he knew you had got back all right.' His steady gaze made her flush and she looked down at the white sheepskin rug, tongue-tied. They stood in silence for what seemed an eternity, then Rafael touched her arm lightly.

'Come on, I'll walk you to your room.' His voice was soft and even. Lila thought she detected a hint of disappointment in his tone. She herself was experiencing a painful mixture of embarrassment, relief, and letdown. Even now, she knew, if he took her in his arms again she would find it impossible to push him away. Never before had she thought of herself as a passionate woman, but Rafael had revealed to her a new dimension of her being. For the first time she was aware of the demands of her body, and she was frightened by their insistent power.

As Rafael paused outside her bedroom door, her pulse raced. 'I'll be gone by the time you're down for breakfast,' he whispered, 'so I'll say goodbye now.' His lips brushed hers briefly, then he opened the bedroom door behind her.

Lila tried to wish him well, but found herself unable to utter a sound, and retreated hastily into her room. Her chin was trembling uncontrollably and her eyes stung with sudden tears. 'Too much has happened to me today,' she said aloud, as if to reassure herself that she had no other cause to be upset.

Her bandaged ankle, although clumsy, had grown less painful, and Lila was able to prepare for bed without difficulty. The cool sheets soothed her skin, which still burned from Rafael's caresses. In the dark her mind raced uncontrollably and she wondered if she would ever sleep. Was Rafael a man who easily pretended tenderness in order to have his way with women? Had she so nearly succumbed to a well-practised routine? A routine that women like Stephanie were undoubtedly familiar with, she thought bitterly. Rafael seemed more enigmatic than ever. Why had he taken her back to her room, when he must have known how easy it would have been to persuade her to remain with him? Perhaps he had already lost what little interest he had in her. Probably she had been too easy, although Rafael surely expected no more than that from an artist.

Tossing restlessly between the sheets, ignoring the repeated twinges of pain from her ankle, Lila tormented herself with her thoughts. Not until the sky was beginning to turn grey with dawn did she finally fall asleep. She woke up suddenly two hours later at the sounds of Carlos calling, *'Adios!'* and the engine of the Mercedes rumbling below. So Rafael was already leaving. A single tear rolled off her cheek as she buried her face miserably in the down pillow.

CHAPTER NINE

ONCE she had forced herself to dress and go downstairs, Lila's energy seemed to be exhausted. Maria, noticing the dark circles under her eyes, immediately assumed that her sleepless night had been caused by her painful ankle. She insisted on pampering her by settling her on the veranda, and propping her foot on soft pillows. She gathered a selection of books and magazines which were scattered about the house and put them on a table beside her. After the rain, the sky was clear with but a few fluffy clouds, and the air had a refreshing bite. Lila dozed peacefully in her chair, oblivious to Carlos' and Maria's careful whispers and tiptoeing.

After lunch she treated herself to a short walk in front of the house, aided by Carlos' sturdy shoulder. Although she limped slightly, she thought she was improving enough to be able to return soon to the ruins. She still had work left to do, she reminded herself sternly. As she and Carlos were proceeding slowly up the front steps, a pale green Mercedes pulled into the driveway. As they turned to watch, a grey-haired woman in a stylish linen dress got out of the car and approached them, a puzzled frown on her tanned forehead.

'Who is she, Carlos?' Lila whispered.

'I've seen her before, but I don't remember her name,' Carlos replied unhelpfully.

Lila tried frantically to remember if she had been introduced to the woman at a party or the fiesta. No, she had no recollection of having seen her before, she decided as the woman came closer. 'I beg your pardon. I was looking for Stephanie Marshall.'

'She's not here now,' Lila replied, hardly knowing how to answer.

'Do you know when she will be back?' the woman asked, consulting her small gold locket watch. Lila looked helplessly at Carlos. She knew nothing about Stephanie's plans.

'She's not here at all,' Carlos supplied vaguely. 'She went back home on the plane.'

'Oh, dear!' Her soft round face was lined with vexation. 'I was counting on Stephanie to help me. Now I don't know what I'm going to do.'

'I'm Lila Fleming.' Lila paused. 'Perhaps there's something I can do,' she suggested, responding to the woman's distress.

'Well, I don't know,' she responded absently, seeming confused.

'Why don't you come inside out of the heat?'

They sat down in the sunny living room and Carlos went to ask Maria for some iced tea.

'I'm Gladys Bingham. Please call me Gladys,' the visitor said. 'I don't really know how to begin.

You see, Stephanie was to help me with our benefit auction. It's only ten days away now.' The puzzled look returned to her face. 'She seemed like a responsible young woman. I was sure she'd be almost finished with the task and now I find she apparently hasn't begun. I don't know what to do. I have so many other things to arrange. In fact,' she added briskly, 'where is Mr Blake?'

'He's out of town too,' Lila answered.

'Oh, no!' Gladys put her hand to her forehead. 'We wanted to hold the auction in his big dining room. Stephanie said she would ask him.'

'Maybe if you explained to me what this is for . . .' Lila began, wondering in the back of her mind if Rafael's absence gave her the authority to volunteer the use of his dining room.

'Well,' Gladys began, taking a sip of her iced tea, 'a family in the village—the Nava family—one of the children needs surgery for a crippled leg. The boy and his mother will have to go to the University medical centre in Mexico City and stay for several weeks. Anyway, you see, the family has no money, so we wanted to help. But since *most* people had already donated so much to the clinic, we thought we'd try a different method.'

'I see,' Lila said neutrally. Was Gladys referring to the fact that Rafael had done nothing for the clinic? Despite the fact that Lila herself had criticised him for this, she thought it inappropriate for Gladys to make such a point of it. The implication was, she supposed, that Rafael should do more on this occasion.

'So,' Gladys went on, 'local people will donate items to be auctioned off, and we're hoping to gets lots of tourists from the nearby hotels to come. It's a big job to organise.'

'Can I help in some way?' Lila asked. Since Rafael was gone, it seemed to her that someone should make a contribution in his place, and there seemed to be no one but her to do it.

'Well, Stephanie was going to be in charge of collecting for the auction in the area I've marked on this map.' Gladys rummaged in her purse and drew out a wrinkled map which had been marked in red pencil. 'I've just discovered she hadn't even started on the job, so there's a great deal left to do. Since Stephanie's gone, would you be willing . . .?'

'I would be happy to help,' Lila replied. She had expected to be asked to make posters or do the decorations, but this sounded a lot more interesting. 'I don't have transportation, though,' she remembered suddenly.

'Oh, you can use my car. I'll be so grateful to get the work done.' Gladys gave her a relieved smile. 'After all, we won't have an auction if we don't get plenty of donations.' She stood up, fishing in her purse. 'Here's my phone number. Give me a call tomorrow and I'll bring you the car and get you started.'

She walked briskly to the door as Lila tucked the card in her pocket. 'Oh, I almost forgot, do

you think you can get in touch with Mr Blake
about the dining room? I'm afraid it's the only
place large enough.'

'I'll try,' Lila agreed as her visitor hurried off.
Someone must know how to reach Rafael, although this hardly seemed worth disturbing him
about. Maybe she should just give the permission
herself? It seemed like the right thing to do.
Resolving to sleep on it, Lila limped into the
garden to find Carlos.

'Is that lady gone?' he asked immediately,
wrinkling his nose.

Lila nodded absently. In coming to the house
to look for Stephanie, Gladys had reminded her
that Stephanie's clothes still hung in the closet,
and that she would be coming back. Lila felt a
twinge of despair.

'Does Stephanie spend much time here?' she
asked rather abruptly. Subtlety would probably
be wasted on Carlos, she thought.

'Well,' Carlos replied with a shrug, 'I'm here
only some of the time, so I don't really know.'

'You mean you don't live here?' Lila was
astounded. Somehow it had never occurred to her
that Carlos was just visiting. But once she thought
about it, it seemed clear that he would have a
home and family elsewhere.

'Mostly I live with my grandma.'

'Rafael's mother?' she asked, increasingly
puzzled.

'No, my other grandma. And then on vacations

I stay with Uncle Rafael. My mother was his sister.'

'I see,' Lila responded slowly. It seemed better not to ask more questions about Carlos' family. If his mother had died only recently, it might upset him to talk about it. And Lila knew from her own experience how painful it could be to respond to thoughtless questions.

'I don't think Stephanie likes you very much,' Carlos offered ingenuously, abruptly returning to Lila's original topic.

Lila laughed dryly. 'You could be right about that,' she agreed, and shrugged her shoulders indifferently. Suddenly she didn't want to find out any more about Stephanie. In a few weeks she would be far away and she would never know about Stephanie's return to the house, or whether Rafael married her. And it would make no difference to her even if she did know, she assured herself. Just because she was staying at Rafael's house it did not mean she had a stake in his personal life. And a few kisses, no matter how passionate, did not change that.

Resolutely she pushed Stephanie to the back of her mind. 'Carlos, does Rafael call you when he's away?' If Rafael made regular calls, she could ask him about holding the auction in the dining room.

'He calls sometimes, but not too often,' Carlos replied vaguely.

'Does he leave a telephone number where you could call him?'

Carlos pondered for a moment. 'I think he tells Maria, but I'm not sure.'

'I think I'll check with Maria now,' Lila decided. 'Mrs Bingham wants to hold a benefit auction in the dining room. So I'd like to call your uncle and ask him about it. Do you want to come inside with me?'

'No,' Carlos shook his head energetically. 'It's boring in there.'

Lila found Maria in the kitchen and ascertained that she did indeed know how to reach Rafael. But upon finding that he was several thousand miles away, Lila was less enthusiastic about calling him. It seemed foolish to make such an expensive call over what was really a minor decision. After all, it wasn't as if someone wanted to hold a bullfight in the house. After the auction, the dining room could be restored to its original condition and Rafael would find no cause for complaint.

Maria agreed to help with whatever cleaning up would be required. 'It will be my contribution to the Nava family,' she said proudly. 'They deserve the help, and I'm sure Señor Blake would be pleased to offer his dining room if he knew.'

Maria sounded so convinced that Rafael wouldn't mind that Lila felt reassured about making the decision herself. 'Well,' she answered, 'as long as you don't mind the extra work, I'll tell them to go ahead, and I'll help you with whatever needs to be done. I suppose we'll have to get some strong men to help move the furniture.'

'Leave that part to me,' said Maria, obviously pleased to be given some responsibility in the benefit. 'I'll make sure we have all the help we need.'

Lila called Gladys early the following morning to tell her the news about the dining room. The older woman's obvious pleasure and relief at the news made Lila feel she had made the right choice, and left her with only an occasional twinge of anxiety about whether she was being presumptuous in loaning out Rafael's property. Shortly after the telephone call, Gladys arrived to present Lila with the keys to her car, a map, and a list of names.

'I usually call the people, tell them what we're looking for, and try to set up an appointment for the following day to pick up the donations. That way they don't have time to forget. I've already telephoned these three,' Gladys pointed to three names with checkmarks after them, 'so they're expecting someone.'

Lila took the map and list with some trepidation. The list was a lot longer than she had anticipated. It meant meeting new people every day and she was not sure how good she would be at persuading all these people to donate something. Gladys touched her arm. 'I meant to ask you yesterday, can you manage all this with an injured ankle? I don't want to ask too much of you.'

'It's just a sprain.' Lila shrugged it off. The

bandage was bulky and awkward and she was careful about putting weight on the foot, but the ankle had not hurt her at all since that night. What hurt more was the memory of her body's uninhibited response to a man who cared nothing for her. How could she have betrayed herself by allowing him to discover her readiness to surrender to his sensual powers? As her recollections threatened to bring a blush to her cheeks, she brought her attention back to the present.

'Well, I'll head back home, then. I'm sure you'll do fine,' Gladys added, recognising Lila's sudden nervousness. 'These first ones,' she pointed to the checked names, 'will be no trouble at all.' After offering a few more suggestions on the visits, Gladys left in a rush.

Deciding she might as well take the bull by the horns, Lila went upstairs to dress for her first visits. She could make an early start and see a few people before lunch. Dropping in on people after lunch could be awkward, since many liked to take an afternoon siesta.

Lila's first visit was a breeze, as Gladys had predicted. She approached the small house diffidently, admiring the carefully tended flower beds which bordered the flagstone path to the door. A bright green lawn and neatly trimmed shrubs under the windows reminded her of home. The house hardly seemed to belong in Uxmal at all, she thought as she raised the brass knocker.

Once inside the sunny living room, Lila discovered that the MacHenrys, an elderly couple, had known about the auction for some time and were waiting for someone to stop by. They had already gathered together a number of small items for the auction, including some old family heirlooms that they had decided to dispose of. When Lila exclaimed over a china doll clad in a faded blue satin gown trimmed with exquisite lace, Mrs MacHenry remarked, 'I was saving this for my granddaughter, but it was just foolishness on my part. She has no interest in such things. For her it's motorbikes and skiing.'

'Don't you think she may change her mind later?' Lila asked, remembering her own tomboy days.

'Well, I don't know,' Mrs MacHenry said thoughtfully. 'It's no good trying to make a person be something she's not.'

'But think how disappointed you'll both be if she wants it later and it's gone,' Lila countered.

'She's right, dear,' Mr MacHenry spoke for the first time. 'Why don't we set it aside for a time? We can always give it away to a good cause later.'

As Lila left bearing a collection that did not include the china doll, she ruefully remembered some advice Gladys had given her. 'Don't give them a chance to reconsider, Lila, or you'll end up with nothing. These are mostly older folks on your list and they've become very attached to all their possessions. Even after they decide to part with something, they're likely to change their

minds if you give them an excuse.' Well, Lila
thought, she didn't want to collect things at the
expense of the owner's family. If she had had a
grandmother who had saved such a doll for her,
she would have bitterly resented someone else
talking her grandmother into giving the doll away.
She just hoped Mrs MacHenry's granddaughter
would grow up to treasure the doll as it should
be.

Lila made two more visits, both fairly successful, then stopped when her ankle began to feel a
little tired. She didn't want to keep the bandage
on any longer than necessary, which meant taking
very good care of the sprain. She felt clumsy and
unattractive in the floppy sandal she wore over
the bulky bandage. When she was meeting so
many people for the first time, as she was bound
to in collecting for the auction, she would have
preferred to be at her best. Still, as it turned out,
the bandaged ankle gave people something to ask
her about and had made it much easier to establish
friendly relationships.

Back at the house, she examined her first day's
collection more closely. Someone else would be
cataloguing the items and setting a price on them,
but Lila just enjoyed looking at them. There were
curios from around the world including a brittle
ivory fan, an embroidered lime-green parasol, and
an exquisitely carved jade elephant. There was
also a good assortment of pottery and several
hand-woven baskets. Lila was most interested in

the delicate lace mantillas she had been given at one house. The fine workmanship in one delighted her as she held it up to the light, and she resolved to bid for it. She knew she probably couldn't afford it, but it would make a beautiful wedding veil, she thought wistfully.

Her collection grew as the days passed. She settled into a routine of making several visits in the morning. Then after lunch she and Carlos would take the day's collection to Gladys and return the car. In the afternoons she worked on her paintings, taking time out to make telephone calls from the list Gladys had given her. Those who agreed over the telephone would be visited the following day.

One afternoon when Lila had taken a painting out into the garden to enjoy the cool breeze while she worked she was startled to discover that Carlos had been watching her. Slowly she put her brush down, wondering what to say. She had promised Rafael she would abide by his wishes, but she really didn't have the heart to tell Carlos he had to leave. Pushing her fingers through her hair, she went over and sat down on a nearby lounge chair and invited Carlos to join her.

The boy looked at her soberly as he sat down. He already knew what she was going to say, Lila fretted. 'Carlos,' she began gently, 'I think you know what your uncle has said to me about you and my painting.'

'Yes,' Carlos replied in a near whisper.

'I don't want to go against his judgment,' Lila continued, watching the disappointment grow in the boy's face.

'Uncle Rafael doesn't understand,' Carlos said with tears in his voice. 'He doesn't want me to waste my time on painting, but Lavinia says it's in my blood and it's got to come out.'

'Lavinia? Who's Lavinia?' Lila was bewildered and concerned. It sounded as if someone had been feeding Carlos some sort of superstitions.

'She's my grandmother,' Carlos said with exasperation, as if the fact should be obvious to everyone. 'She likes me to call her Lavinia. She says it makes her feel younger.'

'All right. So what does Lavinia think is in your blood?' Lila was determined to get the whole story, even if she had to extract it bit by bit.

'Art!' Carlos announced, spreading his arms dramatically. 'See,' he continued in a more normal tone, 'my father was an artist. But he died in an automobile accident. My mother was in the car and she died too.' Noticing Lila's look of horror, he hurried to add, 'I was just a baby, so I didn't know. But Lavinia says I'm going to be a painter just like my father, whether Rafael likes it or not. She says Rafael just never thought anyone was good enough for his sister, and that's why he doesn't like artists now. But Rafael says it's more than that, and he'll explain when I'm old enough to understand.'

The simple 'I see' that Lila understandingly

uttered gave no hint of the connections she was busily making in her head. Rafael had already made it clear that he had disapproved of his sister's husband. And though she didn't know which came first—his disapproval of him or his dislike of artists—it was likely that his prejudices against artists were based more on personal than philosophical grounds. Maybe his experiences with Carlos' father had convinced him that no one could be a productive member of society and an artist too. The death of his sister must have been a terrible blow to him. She didn't know if what she had heard made his attitudes any less infuriating, but it did help her to understand one little piece of the enigma known as Rafael Blake. In any event, she still had Carlos to cope with right now.

'Well, no matter what your grandmother has said, when you stay with Rafael you must obey him. And so must I,' she added, nearly choking on the words. 'I've finished painting for today, but after this you mustn't come around when I'm working. Is it a deal?' she finished lightly, tousling his hair.

'Okay.' Carlos seemed resigned as they went in to dinner.

The following morning came Lila's last visits, including one Lila had been dreading. It was a Miss Burkett, who according to Gladys had no telephone. She had said, 'It's probably a waste of time to go there. I wouldn't have put her name

on the list, but she does have a house packed to
the rafters with treasures.' Gladys said this Miss
Burkett was a very isolated old lady who did not
participate in local affairs. No one knew much
about her, except that she was not receptive to
visitors. She had a maid who did her shopping
for her, so she was rarely seen at all. 'However,'
Gladys concluded with a grimace, 'I hear she has
dozens of cats to keep her company, so perhaps
she's not lonely at all.'

Lila was tempted to skip Miss Burkett alto-
gether, but she decided she might as well try.
After all, the old lady would only send her away
empty-handed, and she would be no worse off
than when she started. She looked in the closet
with a frown of disapproval. None of her dresses
was really appropriate for morning wear, and she
could guess that Miss Burkett was the type who
did not approve of slacks. But there was really
nothing to be done, except to dress as neatly as
possible. She settled on her yellow slacks and
white eyelet blouse. Twisting her hair up neatly
into a knot, she decided she looked as prim as she
could hope to.

Miss Burkett's house was a small white adobe
structure surrounded by a low adobe wall with a
gently curving top. Gladys had said it was a very
old building which had most recently housed the
village teacher. Lila walked through an entryway
cut into the wall into a yard overgrown with suc-
culents and vines. She could hear a strange mix-

ture of noises which appeared to be coming from the house—the frenzied yelping of at least one dog, several people shouting, birds squawking angrily, and what sounded like someone pounding on a tin pan. Lila rapped on the front door several times, with little hope she would be heard. Eventually she peered through the front window and saw that the dim interior of the house was empty.

Having come this far, Lila decided she might as well go around to the back of the house and at least find out what was going on. Stepping gingerly through the overgrown yard, she rounded the corner of the house and gave a short burst of laughter at the spectacle that met her eyes. A tiny, wizened Indian woman was clutching desperately at a lunging, yelping mongrel puppy. Nearby, an equally ancient woman held a pot and spoon above her head and was banging them together vigorously. A few feet above her a small cat clung to a branch of the fruit tree, meowing pitifully. Several birds flapped overhead, apparently trying to drive the cat away. As the women caught sight of Lila, both stopped what they were doing and a brief silence ensued.

The puppy immediately rushed to the tree and began whining and scrabbling at the trunk. 'Would you like me to get the cat out of the tree?' Lila asked, realising what was causing all the commotion.

'That would be very kind of you,' the old lady

replied sedately. 'There's a bird's nest up there and I don't want Lucifer to get into it. I was banging the pan to scare him down, but it didn't work.'

Lila set down her handbag and removed her sandals. Climbing the tree shouldn't be too difficult if she could achieve the lower branch. Even with the puppy underfoot, she managed to pull herself up. After moving up a few more branches, she saw the cat within reach and grabbed him quickly under his front legs. Climbing back down with the cat kicking frantically against her grip was less easy, and she was relieved to finally feel her feet touch the ground. Miraculously, her ankle had not given her a twinge.

Excited by the closeness of the cat, the puppy began leaping at her legs, covering her slacks with paw marks. The cat jumped out of her arms, leaving a long red scratch down one arm. Lila could feel her hair coming loose and falling into her face as she put her shoes on.

'Would you care for a cup of coffee?' the lady who must be Miss Burkett asked politely.

'That would be lovely,' Lila replied, trying ineffectually to straighten her hair.

The living room was so crowded with collector's items of every description that Lila had some difficulty finding a place to sit. As she sipped at her coffee, she explained to Miss Burkett the purpose of her visit.

'Well,' the old lady said dubiously, 'I don't

usually participate in this kind of thing. I keep to myself. That's what I was taught. As for donations, if I didn't want these things,' her gesture taking in the entire room, 'I wouldn't have them in the first place.'

Although she had been prepared for a refusal, Lila could not help feeling disappointed. 'I see,' she said in a low voice. 'Well, I won't take up any more of your time, then,' and returned her cup to its saucer in preparation for leaving.

'Since you helped me with the cat,' Miss Burkett said, apparently re-evaluating her position, 'I guess I should try to find one or two things for your auction.' She stood up and looked vaguely around the room.

'That would be very nice of you,' Lila replied, 'but it's really not necessary.' She almost bit her tongue, remembering too late that it really was important to get as many items as possible for the auction.

Miss Burkett was busy in a dim corner, seemingly stacking and rearranging a crowd of mysterious objects in a bookshelf. 'Well, I don't enjoy this much any more,' she said abruptly, and handed Lila a dusty antique paperweight. 'You can have this, too, if you want,' she added, offering an intricately carved ivory letter-opener.

In the end, Lila almost filled the back of the car with Miss Burkett's donations. While thanking the old lady for the last time, she noticed that the living room seemed just as crowded as it had when she arrived. Flushed with triumph, she returned to Gladys's house to present her with the latest acquisitions.

'You're a miracle worker!' Gladys exclaimed when she saw what was in her car. 'What did you have to do—fight for these things?' she asked, taking in Lila's dishevelled condition.

'Not really,' Lila laughed.

'Don't you want to tidy up here before you go home?'

Lila inspected her soiled clothes and made an ineffectual attempt to straighten her hair. 'I think I'd better just go home, take a shower, and change,' she answered. 'Let me know what else I can do for the benefit.'

'There's sure to be more, but you deserve this afternoon off.' Gladys was busy examining the new donations and waved rather absentmindedly as Lila left for Palmera House.

CHAPTER TEN

LILA walked briskly to the house, hoping no one she knew would see her when she was so scratched and dirty. She went straight to her room and opened the door, completely unprepared for the sight of Stephanie standing in front of the closet, hands on her hips.

'Can I help you find something?' Lila asked coldly, as she saw Stephanie begin to rifle through her clothes in the closet.

Stephanie turned slowly. 'Oh, it's you,' she remarked disdainfully. 'I see you've taken over my room.'

Lila was taken aback. 'I'm sorry. Is this your room?' If it was Stephanie's, why had Rafael put her here? Stephanie's clothes had been hanging in the closet. That should have told her something about whose room this was.

'Does Rafael know you're here?' Stephanie asked, her eyes narrowing suspiciously.

'Of course he does. He invited me here,' Lila replied, trying unsuccessfully not to sound defensive. What right did Stephanie have just to march into her bedroom and interrogate her?

'Well,' said Stephanie, giving a short humourless laugh, 'ordinarily I would be jealous at Rafael having invited a female guest to Palmera. I guess under the circumstances, I have nothing to worry about.' She appraised Lila's soiled clothing and unkempt hair.

Lila blushed, suddenly remembering how she looked. Somehow Stephanie always caught her at her worst. Stephanie, of course, looked stunning in a jade green linen suit and white silk blouse. 'Yes, well, I was planning to bathe and change.'

'I'll be going to another room as soon as I'm sure I have all my dresses,' Stephanie replied smoothly, seemingly restored to a semblance of civility.

Lila stood awkwardly by while Stephanie examined every hanger in the closet. At last, with her own dresses hung over one arm, Stephanie carelessly pushed Lila's clothes aside. 'Oh my, what have we here?' she exclaimed dramatically, sliding Lila's portrait of Rafael out of the closet and propping it up on the dresser.

Oh no! Lila groaned to herself. Next to Rafael, Stephanie was about the last person she would have wanted to find her painting. What was more, Stephanie would probably tell Rafael and the secret would be out.

Stephanie backed away as if to appraise the portrait. 'That's Rafael, isn't it? I'm surprised he was willing to pose. He's not usually interested in amateur endeavours.'

Lila was seething by now. Not only had

Stephanie invaded her privacy, she was insulting her work.

'It's not bad, really,' Stephanie remarked condescendingly. 'At least I could tell who it was.' She glanced at Lila curiously. 'You don't like my looking at it, do you?'

'I wasn't planning to display it,' Lila replied ambiguously.

'Well, I must be going. I have a million things to do,' Stephanie announced, sounding, as if she were leaving an afternoon tea party. She glanced back at Lila as she was halfway out of the door. 'We'll talk again about your visit here,' she said, her voice suddenly hard. 'I'm interested to hear just how you came to be here. But I won't keep you any longer now. I'm sure you want to tidy up,' she said with a false smile. 'I'll be moving in to the room next door to Rafael.'

Lila sighed as she finally closed the door behind the brunette. She undressed slowly and stepped into her bath, her mind on Stephanie's reappearance. Why had Rafael put her in Stephanie's room? It must have occurred to him that she would not be pleased to find Lila living in the house. It seemed clear that Stephanie had become almost a permanent resident of Rafael's house. No doubt they would marry eventually, Lila thought, attributing the burning in her eyes to some stray soapsuds. Somehow, she would not have thought Rafael the kind of man who would make love to one woman when he was committed to another.

But, she reminded herself bitterly, since she was an artist he probably considered her fair game.

Her bath water had grown cold before she stepped out on to the thick terrycloth mat. As she dried herself with an oversized sky-blue towel, she realised that her leisurely pace was in part due to her reluctance to face Stephanie again. But she couldn't stay in her room all afternoon, and in any case she had promised Carlos a game of checkers. After dressing in her tangerine pants and white blouse, she pulled her hair back in a tortoiseshell clip and went downstairs to find Carlos.

The afternoon passed quickly for Lila, divided as it was between Carlos and her painting. She had managed to push Stephanie's presence out of her mind, until she went in to dinner and found her already seated at the table. Her pale blue eyes were searing with anger and her lips were tightly compressed. As soon as Lila sat down, Stephanie launched into what was obviously a prepared speech.

'It's one thing to move into my room when I'm gone, but it's quite another to usurp my role in the auction. When I called Gladys Bingham, she told me you had already done the job I was to do.' She set down her water glass with a loud thud. 'I hadn't planned on leaving at all, but my lawyer seemed to consider it vital that I appear in court for my divorce. I returned as quickly as possible just so I could do that job,' she added, glaring at Lila.

Lila was both surprised and embarrassed. 'Gladys was so worried that the job wouldn't get done, and no one knew when you were coming back,' she said apologetically. 'And really,' she continued reasonably, 'there are only two days left until the auction. I've spent a week on the job and I just finished today.'

'I'm sure I could have finished in plenty of time,' Stephanie snapped, tapping her knife impatiently on her plate.

'Well, I'm very sorry,' Lila murmured, twisting her napkin fiercely under the table. 'I had no idea. . . .'

'Don't think you can fool me so easily! I'm sure you know very well that Rafael fancies himself an old-fashioned lord of the manor. He considers these kinds of benefits very important. And you think you can get into his good graces by helping with the auction.' Stephanie made a grimace. 'Rafael considers it everyone's duty to help those who are less fortunate. That's why he gave such a ridiculously large sum of money to the free medical clinic.'

Her voice continued, but Lila no longer heard her. So Rafael was the anonymous donor who had funded the clinic! And she, in her ignorance, had accused him of doing nothing to help others. No wonder he had been so angry with her! She almost squirmed with embarrassment at the memory of all she had said to him at the fiesta.

With a start she realised that Stephanie's voice

was rising. 'And however you tricked him into letting you stay here, I hope you realise it was just another of his charitable acts. He's rather gullible in some ways, but I'm not. So don't think your plan to impress him by running around doing good works is going to succeed. I'll see that he learns the truth!'

There seemed very little she could say in reply to Stephanie's speech, so Lila sat quietly, toying with her food. Glancing across the table at Carlos, she saw that he was wriggling miserably in his chair, his dinner barely touched.

'Can I be excused?' he blurted out when Lila caught his eye.

'Of course,' said Lila, at the same time hearing Stephanie's emphatic, 'Certainly not!'

'I'm afraid this conversation is very unpleasant for Carlos,' Lila said, trying to intercede for him.

'Well,' Stephanie replied haughtily, 'if this is the most unpleasant experience he has in his life, I'll be surprised. He has to learn some time to tolerate differences of opinion.' Turning to Carlos, she said, 'As our host, you should stay at the table until we've finished. You're going to have a lot of responsibilities when you grow up. It's time you started learning how to carry them out.'

As Carlos stared dejectedly into his lap, Lila pushed her plate aside. Why did Stephanie insist on involving Carlos in this situation? It was unfair to make him feel he had to stay and listen. She could see only one way to save him further discomfort.

'I have some business to take care of this evening, and it's getting late. So if you'll excuse me, I'll be on my way.' Without waiting to hear Stephanie's reply, Lila walked briskly out the door and unconsciously headed in the direction of Gladys Bingham's house. She really had no reason to go there, but maybe she could help do something for the auction. She simply could not stay in the house another minute with Stephanie.

Gladys seemed pleased, if surprised, to see her. 'Come and have some iced tea with me,' she invited. When they were comfortably seated on her brick patio, Gladys adopted a more serious expression. 'I'm afraid I put you in an awkward position by asking you to do Stephanie Marshall's job. When I talked to her on the phone today, she seemed quite upset.' Gladys stirred sugar into her iced tea with what seemed unnecessary briskness. 'She never could have done the job in the time there is left. And frankly, even if she had all the time in the world, she could never have got as much co-operation as you have.'

Lila flushed with pleasure. 'I'm glad you think so. It's true that Stephanie is pretty angry.'

Gladys gave her a searching look. 'It must be difficult, with the two of you in Palmera together.'

'Yes, it is,' Lila admitted. She gave a short humourless laugh. 'Stephanie doesn't think I should be there at all.' She sipped slowly at her tea, relieved to find someone she could talk over her problems with.

'Have you thought of moving out?' Gladys asked neutrally.

'Yes, in fact I was thinking about it on the way over tonight. But I'll only be here a few more days, so it hardly seems worthwhile. Besides, I've made commitments to help with the auction, and I promised Rafael I'd keep Carlos company.'

'Yes, I don't imagine Stephanie would be interested in offering him much company,' Gladys agreed. 'Do you expect Rafael to return before you leave?'

'I don't know when he's coming back,' Lila admitted, carefully removing a tiny spider from her knee. She looked up to find Gladys studying her closely and lowered her eyes.

'Well, in any case,' said Gladys with an encouraging smile, 'there's no reason to just abandon the field to Stephanie, is there?'

Lila shook her head emphatically. 'It's not as if Stephanie and I were in competition.'

'Oh, no?' Gladys looked quizzically at Lila, her chin resting on her hand.

'No, not at all,' Lila said vehemently, suddenly feeling it was time she left. 'I'm just here for a brief visit. And anyway,' she paused, 'Rafael would never be seriously interested in someone like me.'

'Well,' Gladys concluded with a soft smile, 'I won't pester you about it any more. But there's one thing I've noticed. You haven't said that you could never care for someone like Rafael.'

Lila swirled the remaining inch of iced tea in her glass to hide her confusion. It was true that she could easily imagine falling in love with Rafael. But that would obviously be foolish. A man of Rafael's charm and experience would quickly forget the few passionate moments he and she had shared. For herself, Lila had to admit, it was different. No man had ever affected her the way Rafael did, and the memory of their times together was permanently etched in her memory. But it was important to keep in mind that he had never pretended to care for her. What little interest he had in her was purely physical. It would be best, she concluded, if Rafael did not return before it was time for her to leave.

She glanced up at Gladys, who was regarding her with sympathy. 'If I were you,' Gladys offered, 'I wouldn't give up without a fight.'

'It's a lost cause,' Lila replied with a sigh, and stood up to leave.

'I'll probably see you tomorrow,' Gladys said as Lila left. 'I want to take a look at the dining room and see how many chairs it will hold.'

Lila felt her steps slow the closer she came to Palmera. If she were lucky, maybe she would be able to avoid Stephanie for the rest of the evening. Finding Carlos sitting on the front step she paused, wrinkling her nose at his sullen expression.

'Stephanie's gone to some kind of party,' he announced.

'You seem pretty unhappy,' Lila commented. 'Did you want her to stay here tonight?'

'No,' Carlos replied without meeting Lila's eyes. 'I just want her to go far away and not come back. She keeps telling me how I'll have to act when she's in charge.'

'Well,' Lila said thoughtfully, resting her hand on Carlos's shoulder, 'there's no point in making yourself miserable over something that may never happen.'

Carlos glanced up briefly, and Lila saw that his eyes were full of tears. 'Come on,' she said briskly, starting up the steps. 'Since we have the evening to ourselves, let's play some checkers.'

Stephanie did not return to the house before Lila fell asleep, nor did she appear at breakfast the following morning. According to Maria, she had come in quite late. Hoping that Stephanie would manage to sleep through lunch, Lila went to the garden to put some finishing touches on her paintings. Actually, she knew, it was time she stopped fiddling with them, but when she had the time it was hard to resist the temptation to correct a few problems. And then each time she looked at them she found more things to fix.

Lila was preparing to put her things away for lunch, when Maria came to tell her she was wanted on the phone. She hurried into the house for a brief conversation with Gladys, who wanted to set a time to look over the dining room. Returning to the garden, she saw Stephanie apparently rearranging and stacking her paintings. Lila felt her heart lurch.

'Be careful!' she called sharply. 'The paint is still wet on some of those.'

Stephanie winced and put her hands over her ears, letting one painting drop to the ground. 'Don't raise your voice!' she hissed irritably. 'I've got the world's worst hangover.'

Coming closer, Lila saw that Stephanie's eyes were a mass of red lines and her complexion pasty. Silently she organised her paintings and prepared to carry the two she had recently worked on back to her room.

'Quite the busy bee, aren't we?' Stephanie remarked, massaging her temples with her fingertips.

'Painting is what I came here to do,' Lila replied.

'But you're not averse to snaring a husband on the side,' Stephanie retorted bitingly.

Lila struggled to maintain her composure. 'I'm afraid you have the wrong idea about that,' she replied as evenly as she could, then turned quickly and carried the paintings back to her room. When she returned to the garden for the rest of her things, Stephanie had disappeared, much to Lila's relief.

Lunch was surprisingly pleasant. Stephanie put in a brief appearance, drank a glass of iced tea, and went back to her room without a word. Lila noted unsympathetically that her face looked quite green. Immediately after lunch, Lila and Maria began making plans for the use of the dining room.

The oak table was massive, but could probably be moved to one end of the room to display the auction items. The large mahogany china cupboard was also very heavy, but Maria was confident that if it were empty, several men could move it as far as the kitchen. Lila and Maria set to work removing the china, crystal, and silver from the cupboard. Maria had made space in several kitchen cabinets, so Lila nervously carried the delicate pieces into the other room.

The only remaining large piece was an ornately carved linen chest which stood in one corner. Inside, Lila found some old silver utensils with tortoiseshell handles and stacks of starched linen napkins. Removing these items to an available kitchen cabinet, she stood in the doorway and surveyed the room. If the furniture were out, little would remain but several rather traditional paintings on the walls. Gladys could decide about those later, Lila told herself.

When Gladys arrived with her tape measure, she was openly pleased at the size of the room, 'You know,' she told Lila with a slight grimace, 'I've never been in this room before. I'd heard about it, so I decided it would be perfect for the auction. Then I thought, what if someone just exaggerated when they described the room!

So I wanted to come see for myself.'

She chewed thoughtfully on a red fingernail. 'If we use the front door, we can put ropes up so people will come straight in here without disturbing anything. I've arranged for folding chairs. All we need now is something to display the items on before the auction.'

'We were thinking that we could move this table up to one end of the room and turn it sideways . . .' Lila suggested.

'That's wonderful,' Gladys agreed. 'I'll bring some heavy tablecloths to protect it. We'll be serving drinks and canapés before the auction, but Mrs Bennett will bring everything that's needed. We'll easily have room for a small bar at the other end of the room.'

Gladys left, obviously satisfied, and Lila went to the kitchen to confer with Maria. They decided to go ahead and move the furniture that day. The auction was only two days away, and they did not want to find out at the last minute that they needed more help with the preparations. As Maria went off to round up her helpers, Lila sank into a chair.

She was beginning to be nervous about having loaned out Rafael's dining room without his knowledge. With all the furniture being moved around, and all the strangers that would be in the house, it would be easy for something to go wrong. Something of Rafael's could be broken, or even stolen. And Lila would be responsible. Of course, she would pay him for any damage that was done, since she had assumed the responsibility. It would probably take her years to pay for any of his items, but it wasn't that that was bothering her so much. It was really his anger she feared. It was entirely possible that she had once again made a decision he would disapprove of.

Stephanie would undoubtedly have something unpleasant to say about the auction being held in the dining room. Not to mention how she would react to its being done on Lila's authority. And Gladys, Lila suddenly realised, probably just assumed she had called Rafael and obtained his permission. Well, she would have to set Gladys straight right away, to save her possible embarrassment in the future.

Maria reappeared with six husky young men, whom she ordered around very freely. Within a few minutes, the dining room was almost devoid of furniture, and the big table had been positioned at one end. The young men disappeared, one of them offering Lila a grin and a salute just before he went through the door.

'What in the world is going on?' At the sound of Stephanie's voice behind her, Lila gave an involuntary sigh.

'Is Maria planning to wax the floor or something?' Stephanie went on.

'No,' said Lila, resigned to what was to come. 'The benefit auction is going to be held here.'

'Well, I must say that's typical of Rafael—offering his house without giving a thought to the inconvenience it might cause him. But surely he won't be back in time to play host to the auction.' Stephanie flicked the air with her fingers as if drying her nail polish.

'I'm not sure,' Lila answered slowly. 'You see, I'm the one who gave permission for the auction to be here.' She looked nervously aside as Stephanie's eyebrows almost disappeared into her hairline.

'I can see it's time we had a real heart-to-heart talk,' Stephanie said coldly. She turned on her heel and walked into the next room, expecting Lila to follow. After both were seated. Stephanie leaned back and placed her laced fingers under her chin. Lila nervously twisted a handkerchief she had found in her pocket. While Stephanie certainly had some justice on her side in the incipient conversation, she was sure her approach would be both unpleasant and unfair.

'You've taken a great deal on yourself,' Stephanie began bitterly. 'In fact, it would appear that you've taken over the whole household. And, of course, you expect to take over Rafael too. I'm telling you now, I won't let that happen.'

'Things are not at all what you think,' Lila began earnestly.

'Are you trying to pretend he's never even kissed you?' Stephanie asked incredulously. At Lila's deep blush, Stephanie jumped up indignantly. 'I *knew* it! You won't get away with this, so don't even try!'

With those parting words, she flounced out of the room. Lila felt bewildered and humiliated, most of all because she had allowed Stephanie to trick her into revealing some of what had transpired between her and Rafael. Stephanie clearly saw Lila as a rival, and she would probably become increasingly spiteful. It seemed inconceivable to Lila that the worldly, sophisticated Stephanie, already so firmly ensconced in Rafael's life, would feel threatened by her.

Determining to put all her unpleasant chores behind her, Lila telephoned Gladys to tell her that Rafael had never been informed about the dining room. After a long pause, Gladys said forthrightly, 'Ordinarily I wouldn't have taken the dining room under these circumstances, but it's too late to change things around now. We'll just have to hope for the best.' Seeming to sense Lila's discomfort, even through the telephone, she added, 'I wouldn't worry about it now, dear. You did what you thought best at the time, and it can't be undone.'

Lila sighed as she put down the telephone. She was filled with foreboding. Since Stephanie's return, her stay in Uxmal had become distinctly unpleasant. Fortunately, she wouldn't be staying much longer. Her paintings were essentially completed and, if it weren't for the auction, she would feel free to leave that very day. Of course in some ways she would be sorry to go. For one thing, it looked as if Rafael would not be back before she left. Once she had returned home, the portrait of him would be all she would have to remind her of their moments together.

The remainder of that day and the next were filled with the bustle of last-minute arrangements. Folding chairs were delivered and velvet ropes put up to guide people from the front door directly to the dining room. Mrs Bennet arrived with two servants to make arrangements for the refreshments, and Maria was in a frenzy of cleaning and polishing. Stephanie was nowhere in evidence, so Lila found herself quite enjoying all the activity.

The day of the auction dawned clear and hot. Lila was so caught up in the excitement that she had little appetite and found it difficult to pass the hours until it was time to dress. Finally, after selecting slacks and a shirt for Carlos to wear, she went to her room to change. She had decided to wear her white square-necked dress. Not that she had much choice, she thought wryly. Still, with her turquoise pendant and earrings it would be just right for the late afternoon. She decided to leave her hair down in its usual style. She removed her cosmetics from the drawer and surveyed her appearance in the mirror. Her complexion was already so glowing with nervous anticipation, she needed little make-up to enhance her features.

Downstairs, guests were already arriving and soon an excited buzz filled the dining room as the guests filed in to examine the items to be auctioned. Lila made no effort to get to the table through the crowd, but noticed from across the room that many of the more prominently displayed items were ones she had collected. She felt proud of the part she had played in the auction and hoped it would produce enough money for whatever the Nava boy needed.

CHAPTER ELEVEN

LILA'S eyes were suddenly drawn, as if by some sixth sense, to the oak door as it opened to admit additional guests. There, towering over those nearby, was Rafael. Her fingers wrapped themselves around her pendant. She hadn't known exactly when to expect him, but it certainly wasn't now, in the midst of the auction. Anxiously studying his face for a clue to his feelings, she could find no hint. If he were angry, he was keeping it well hidden, Lila thought. But she could imagine how he might feel, arriving home from a long trip to find his dining room packed with strangers.

Rafael caught her eyes and began making his way towards her through the crowd. As she looked at his tanned face, she was reminded of the firelight playing on his forehead as he had bent over her reclining shape, and suddenly all the events of that last evening came rushing over her. As he came nearer, Lila felt her knees begin to weaken beneath her. Rafael surely knew the effect he had on her after her near-surrender that night. Would it make him think even less of her than before, or would he perhaps soften his attitude towards her now that he knew how much power he had?

He greeted her with a wry smile. 'I know this can't be a welcome home party for me because no one knew when I was arriving. Maybe you can enlighten me.'

Lila allowed herself to feel slightly relieved. At least he wasn't furious. 'I'm terribly sorry. I know I should have caled you about it,' she began in a rush. 'This is an auction Gladys Bingham organised to benefit the Nava family—the boy needs a lot of surgery. So I told Gladys they could use your dining room. It was the only place large enough to accommodate all these people. I almost called you, but it would have cost a fortune,' she concluded somewhat breathlessly, mentally bracing herself for his response.

'I don't at all mind having the auction in my dining room,' Rafael said slowly, rubbing his forehead with one hand. 'But I do wish you had consulted me. For one thing, it would have spared me the shock of finding all this,' he gestured around the room, 'after fourteen hours of travelling.'

'I know,' Lila said apologetically. She lowered her eyes, fearing he would misinterpret her elation at his moderate reaction.

Lila grimaced involuntarily as Stephanie pushed through the crowd to rest her hand on Rafael's arm. 'Rafael! I had no idea you were back,' she announced dramatically, rising on her toes to kiss his cheek,' Rafael's eyebrows rose fractionally, and Lila tried unsuccessfully to read his expression. If he was glad to see Stephanie, it wasn't obvious. Stephanie turned to Lila with a thin smile, 'I told you Rafael wouldn't like you loaning out his house without permission.' Looking up at Rafael with fluttering lashes, she added sweetly, 'I hope you haven't been too hard on her.'

'What' I'd really like to know——' Rafael began, when Stephanie interrupted.

'Come and say hello to Gladys,' she said, curling her fingers around his arm, and led him off between the small knots of guests.

Stephine's fingers were like talons, Lila thought bitterly, surprised at the depth of her feelings. Somehow Stephanie reasserting her position with Rafael had left her with a leaden feeling. As she stood alone, moving slightly to accommodate the circulating guests, she thought her future had never looked so bleak.

'I don't understand why I should feel this way,' she said to herself. 'I've known from the beginning that he was in love with her, so why do I continue to let myself be tortured by it?' In spite of all her efforts to the contrary, she had let a few passionate kisses get her in beyond her depth, and she was no longer in control of her feelings. It was just like her, she thought, to be in love for the first time, and have it be someone who was already in love with someone else.

Gladys's voice interrupted her thoughts.

'You're off in another world,' she laughed, looking at Lila closely. 'Are you all right?'

'Of course,' Lila replied, trying to recover some
of her previous exuberance.

'Well, I just spoke to Rafael. He doesn't seem
at all upset about the auction. And,' Gladys went
on with twinkling eyes, 'I made sure to tell him
what a wonderful job you did collecting.
Stephanie gave me such an evil look, I was glad
she wasn't holding a carving knife.' She patted
Lila's shoulder reassuringly. 'Remember, I'm
cheering for you!'

Lila smiled weakly. There seemed no point in
trying to deny her feelings to Gladys. Gladys had
seen through her all along, she realised. And perhaps Françoise had too. It was horrible to think
that her attraction to Rafael had been obvious to
everyone but herself. It made her wonder whether
Rafael himself had been aware of it. Lila flushed
at the thought.

'You really are dreamy today,' Gladys commented. 'Actually I came over to ask you if you
could make a record of the winning bids.'

'Oh, I'd be glad to,' Lila replied wanly.

'Just sit at that card table by the French doors
and each winning bidder will come up and give
you his name and where he's staying. Tell them
that they can either pick up their purchases here
after the auction, or we'll take them to their hotel
if they want. You're being a great help,' she
added, as she hurried off.

Lila began making her way to the card table, depositing her untouched sherry on the bar as she passed. She felt somewhat reluctant to undertake this job. Although she would be seated at the table, and thus less visible than the auctioneer standing at his podium, she still would be in full view of the crowd. Being on display always made her selfconscious, but especially now, when she was feeling particularly exposed and vulnerable. Well, she thought, the auction would be over eventually, and then she would be able to find some privacy. In the meantime, perhaps it would help to keep busy.

Once seated at the card table, she noticed Gladys and several other women trying to shepherd the guests to their chairs. As the crowd became more orderly, she was able to see Rafael and Stephanie clearly. Rafael had turned to leave the dining room, but Stephanie had apparently decided to stay. Her face was flushed and her lips were tightly compressed. Lila wondered briefly what she was upset about. When most of the guests were seated, she walked up the side aisle to Lila's card table and paused, a drink in her hand. 'I just *know* you're going to enjoy this,' she told Lila with an artificial smile, and moved off to find a seat. Why would she say something like that? Lila wondered. She was a little troubled at not being able to guess what Stephanie was hinting at, but as the bidding began, the incident left her mind.

Most of the items seemed to be sell well. The atmosphere often became electric when two or more bidders were in fierce competition for the same thing, each bidding the other up. Caught up in the excitement, Lila frequently had to force her attention back to her list of names. The auctioneer kept things moving briskly, so there was a steady procession of successful bidders coming to her table. Several times a small line of two or three people formed in front of the table when the items were selling unusually quickly.

By the time the auctioneer announced the last item, Lila had listed all the winning bidders to that point, so she was able to relax and enjoy the anticipation produced by what the auctioneer referred to as 'a last-minute surprise donation.' Sensitive to the crowd, the auctioneer delayed showing the item for several minutes, whetting the bidders' appetites by reminding them that the best items were always left for last.

Lila's heart lurched into her throat when the auctioneer finally held up the last item. It was her portrait of Rafael! Wanting desperately to reclaim it before it was cold, she thrust out her arm to the auctioneer. His response was to assume she was making the minimum bid, a price so high Lila slumped back into her chair in defeat. There was no way she could afford to buy it back. She sat in a daze, plunged into despair as the bidding continued. She had never meant for others to see this painting, much less buy it. At last the bidding slowed. As the auctioneer announced the final bid, Rafael appeared in the doorway. His face went ashen as he looked towards the podium and saw the painting.

Lila's already heavy heart was stabbed with anguish. She didn't know what to do, she knew only that she could bear no more. She leapt from her chair and escaped through the nearby French doors. She ran around the back of the house and up to her room, where she leaned against the bedroom door and buried her face in her hands. Tears that she had managed to hold back during her escape now gushed through her fingers.

As her tears gradually subsided, she washed her face and tried to force herself to think the situation through. There was little question about how the painting had come to be auctioned off. Stephanie was the only person apart from Lila who knew of its existence. But why would she do such a thing when she knew Lila wanted the painting kept private? That question kept repeating itself in her emotion-racked mind. The only explanation she could come up with was that Stephanie must have seen the painting as some sort of link between Rafael and Lila, and had spitefully taken it. Lila emitted a sound that was half laugh, half sob. If Stephanie only knew, she had nothing whatsoever to worry about. She was already on the inside, while Lila remained on the outside looking in.

In her spite, Stephanie had made certain the painting was permanently lost to Lila. She did not have anywhere near enough money to buy it back, and even if she had, it was possible the painting's new owner would have refused to part with it. After all, he had had to bid fiercely to win it. It was ironic that Lila could take no pleasure in the high value others had placed on the portrait. No one could have valued it more than Lila herself, for whom it would have been the sole memento of the first man she had loved.

She could hardly bear to speculate on how Rafael must have felt, seeing his own likeness being auctioned off to the highest bidder. Under any circumstances, he probably would have thought it impertinent of Lila to paint him without his approval. But to paint him, and then give the painting away to be sold to a complete stranger, all without his permission, would have been thoughtless and insulting. And that must be what he thought Lila had done. Lila was sure he was outraged at the prospect of having his likeness decorating some tourist's living room.

Rafael was above all a man of pride. He valued his privacy, which was probably why he had founded the clinic anonymously. Now it would appear to him that Lila had violated his privacy, which would just be one more black mark on her character as far as he was concerned. Not that she needed another, Lila concluded despairingly. Being an artist was sufficient in itself.

Lila paced the floor of her room, trying to decide what she should do. She really had no further responsibilities in Uxmal. Her work was essentially complete and the auction was over. Rafael had returned from his business trip, so Carlos wasn't lonely any more. In short, there was absolutely no reason for her to stay on in Uxmal. And, of course, there was Stephanie's presence in the house. A lump came to Lila's throat as she remembered Gladys's remark about what she called 'leaving the field to Stephanie'. There had never even been a contest, Lila thought bitterly as she blinked back fresh tears.

Lila opened the drawer of the dresser and removed her airline ticket. To stay longer could only add to her misery, she thought. She had no desire to mope around, trying to avoid Rafael and Stephanie who would doubtless be enjoying their reunion. Only Carlos would be sorry to see her go.

Before going downstairs, she checked her face in the mirror. Red and swollen eyes stared back at her. She held a damp cloth to them for a few moments until her emotional state was a little less obvious. She hoped to be able to call the airlines and change her reservation without seeing anyone, but with so many people in the house it was difficult to be sure of being alone.

Clutching her ticket, she went swiftly downstairs, ducked into Rafael's study, and made her call. Good! There was a seat available on a flight leaving that very night. Gladys would probably agree to drive her to the airport. Once having decided to leave, she wanted to be gone as fast as possible. 'Let them have Palmera all to themselves,' she thought bitterly. 'I'm not going to stay around and watch.' As she completed her reservation, she saw out of the corner of her eye a shadow move across the windows and her heart began to pound. She had the feeling of being surreptitious and had to remind herself she was only using the telephone.

Several hours remained before her flight. Lila knew she would have to say goodbye to Rafael before she left, no matter how painful the experience might be. She suspected it would be the hardest thing she had ever done. But she had nothing to be ashamed of, and she was not going to allow Stephanie to chase her away like a frightened rabbit.

Lila took one last look around the study. Everything in it was a reminder of Rafael—from its masculine austerity, to the portraits of his family, to his mahogany desk. Now that the painting was gone, she would never again have the opportunity to see him sitting behind this desk, his black hair gleaming in the sun.

Her eyes stinging, she headed back to her room to pack. She changed directions abruptly when she heard several voices apparently about to enter the hall, and went through the back of the house. It occurred to her then that this would be her last chance to see the ruins. The sun hadn't yet set, although it was low in the sky. There would be just enough time for one last visit.

She arrived as most of the tourists were leaving for the day, and took her usual spot against a boulder opposite the House of the Dwarf.

'I believe you forgot this,' said an angry male voice from behind her.

Lila's head swung around with a snap to find Rafael impatiently thrusting her plane ticket in front of her. Her heart was thumping against her rib cage as she reached for the ticket with a trembling hand. As he sat down beside her, she froze. She didn't know whether he was angry over her leaving or over the portrait, but she knew she would soon learn the full measure of his fury.

'Well, am I going to get a thank you for the ticket or not?' he demanded, his lips closing in a firm line.

'Thank you,' she said, too nervous to begin the apology she knew he was waiting for.

'I overheard your telephone call,' Rafael continued, his dark eyes only inches away from hers. 'Does this mean you were actually going to sneak out without so much as a goodbye?' He paused, searching the depths of her turquoise eyes. 'That is a habit of yours, now that I think about it.'

'No,' Lila replied, averting her eyes from the intensity of his gaze. 'I was going to come and tell you.'

'Tell me what?' Rafael demanded, his voice a little louder. 'That you were leaving?'

'Yes. I can't stay here any longer,' she responded, a note of desperation in her voice. She felt she could no longer bear his interrogation.

As she pulled her feet under her to stand up, Rafael's hands gripped her shoulders, commanding her to stay where she was.

'I can think of things I'd rather hear,' he said huskily, and he drew her roughly across his lap. As he lowered his face to hers, Lila closed her eyes, no longer able to trust her senses. 'I'd rather hear how much you love me,' he murmured, his lips so close that she could feel them moving as he spoke.

She moaned aloud as his lips pressed against hers. They both knew that she could not resist his caresses, but it was cruel of him to taunt her with his knowledge. Rafael nuzzled her neck, as his hand moved lightly over her trembling body, dwelling at the curves of her breasts. His fingers left a trail of fire everywhere they touched and her breath was coming in soft gasps. Feeling helplessly adrift, she pulled his mouth to hers, opening her lips to bring him closer. Rafael kissed her tenderly, exploring her depths. She felt his chest rising and falling in a pace quickened by his passion.

He pulled away with a long shuddering breath. 'Look at me,' he commanded. Hesitantly, Lila opened her eyes to meet his gaze. His dark eyes were gleaming, and his usually neat hair was alluringly tousled. Lila thought he had never looked more handsome, and the pain of knowing how soon she would be leaving him filled her eyes with tears.

'Can you pretend now that you don't love me?' Rafael asked harshly, his fingers gripping her chin as she tried to turn her face away.

'You're heartless,' Lila protested, angrily brushing away a warm tear that spilled down her cheek. 'How can you do this when you know you don't care for me at all?'

'You artists,' he replied with a grin, kissing her softly on the nose, 'always think you know everything.' As Lila gazed at him in bewilderment, he went on, 'While I was away, I had plenty of time to think. And for the most part, I thought about you. In fact,' he said emphatically, pulling her up to sit beside him, 'I couldn't get my mind off you.'

'So I asked myself why I kept thinking about you, and I was forced to conclude that I had fallen in love with you. There were only a couple of questions that remained. One was whether you could return my feelings. And when I saw the portrait, I knew the answer to that one.'

Lila stared at him in bewilderment, unable to believe what she had heard. Surely Rafael was not the kind of man to joke about such a subject. Still, his change of heart seemed so sudden to her, she couldn't take it in. 'You said there were a couple of remaining questions. What's the second one?' she asked hesitantly.

Rafael's eyes looked directly into hers. 'The

second one is, what about this boy-friend of yours? I intend to be quite selfish with the woman I love. I don't intend to share, Lila.'

If she weren't so overcome with tenderness and love, she could have been amused by the idea of Steve as her boy-friend. As it was, she simply said, 'Steve is not my boy-friend. I met him on the plane coming here, and he was kind enough to give me a tour of the ruins. We were having lunch after that tour when you saw us.' Lila smiled up at him. 'And now you know all there is to know about me and my "boy-friend".'

'That sounds pretty innocent for an artist,' he teased, 'but I guess I'll have to believe you.'

'That reminds me. I thought you hated artists. So how can you be in love with one?'

His arm tightened around her shoulders. 'Does it matter very much that I'm prejudiced against artists?' he asked playfully.

'Of course,' Lila replied definitely. 'I'm an artist, and you've held that against me from the beginning.'

'I'll try to mend my ways,' Rafael promised with a grin. Pulling her closer, he took her face in his hands and looked at her with serious eyes. 'You know, my brother-in-law was terribly irresponsible. He made my sister miserable while she was alive, and I hold him accountable for her death, for leaving Carlos an orphan. It was from him and his artist friends that I got my ideas about the morality of artists. I admit I've been unreasonable about you.' He paused, studying her turquoise eyes. 'Once we're married, perhaps you can reform me.'

'Married?' Lila cried. 'But what about Stephanie?'

Rafael stiffened and pulled away slightly, and Lila felt her own muscles tense. 'What in the world does Stephanie have to do with it? Do you want her blessing?'

The idyll was over and now they would have another of their familiar battles. For a while, the world had been a lovely, exciting place where dreams came true, but now she was back to reality. 'Stephanie apparently lives with you much of the time,' she began nervously, betraying herself by a stammer. 'When she goes away, she leaves her clothes in the closet. And she said the two of you plan to marry,' she concluded in a rush, dreading his reply. Sometimes the truth was better left unexposed.

Rafael gave a short, angry laugh. 'Stephanie was a childhood friend of my sister's. In fact, they were inseparable for a time. So when she wrote and asked if she could spend part of her vacation here, I agreed. She claimed she needed to get away from some personal problems but couldn't afford to stay at a hotel. I began to suspect there was more on her mind than a vacation, so I was quite relieved when she left.'

'You mean you didn't know she was coming back?'

'I had no idea! She knew I wasn't pleased to see her, but I still didn't turn her out of the house. Then I started asking questions to find out how my portrait came to be auctioned off, and I found out she had stolen your painting. I've just told her to pack her bags. Surely.' Rafael's eyebrow was raised, 'you didn't imagine there was anything between us?'

'Well,' Lila responded, choosing her words carefully, 'the evidence did seem to point that way.'

'You must have noticed, Lila, that Stephanie does not have what one could call a generous spirit. Did you really believe I could be in love with a woman like that?'

'She's very glamorous,' Lila protested.

Rafael smiled suddenly, making Lila's heart turn over. He pulled her close and she nestled her head against his shoulder, feeling perfectly safe and secure. 'You, my love,' he whispered, 'have a beauty all your own, far deeper than can be attained by a glamorous exterior. You are a true woman, warm and giving, and I intend to protect you and make you happy for the rest of your life.'

Lila gazed at him wonderingly, lightly tracing with her fingers the planes of his face. 'I don't think I could ever be happier than I am right now. Everything would be absolutely perfect, if only . . .' She looked down at her feet as the memory of her lost portrait of Rafael darkened her mood. She didn't want Rafael to read her thoughts, and regretted that she had allowed an unpleasant idea to spoil their blissful moment.

Rafael tilted her face up with his fingers and looked searchingly into her eyes as Lila tried to overcome her sudden depression. Before, she had valued the portrait as her only memento of Rafael. But now that she was secure in his love, the portrait seemed all the more precious. Wouldn't it have been a perfect reminder of their meeting and their early misunderstandings? And, without even knowing it herself, she had painted it with love in every brush stroke.

'Tell me,' Rafael demanded softly. 'I won't have this evening marred by anything.'

'Your portrait,' Lila answered simply, gesturing helplessly with her hands.

'Is that all?' Rafael asked, and gave a hearty laugh. 'Well, we can solve that problem very simply. You must have guessed I wouldn't care to have such a thing fall into the hands of strangers. So I managed to persuade the new owner to return it to me. It was to be my wedding gift to you. You will marry me, won't you?' he asked, suddenly serious.

'Yes, of course,' Lila replied, as he pulled her to her feet.

He reached into his shirt pocket and removed a red velvet pouch. Inside was the golden brooch that was to be passed down to each of the women chosen by a Blake.

Lila exclaimed delightedly, 'Oh, Rafael! It's so beautiful!'

'It's been in my family for several generations, and I hope the tradition of giving it to each new bride will continue for many generations to come,' Rafael said seriously. Then a mischievous smile curved his lips. 'Shall we go and tell Carlos? I'm sure he would love to have a small cousin or two to play with.' Laughing at her blushes, he led her back to Palmera.

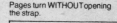